THE DAY THE SCREENS WENT BLANK

Also by Danny Wallace

Hamish and the Worldstoppers

Hamish and the Neverpeople

Hamish and the GravityBurp

Hamish and the Babyboom

Hamish and the Monster Patrol

Hamish and the Terrible Terrible
Christmas and other Starkley Stories

THE DAY THE SCREENS WENT BLANK

DANNY WALLACE

Illustrated by *gemma* CORRELL

SIMON & SCHUSTER

First published in Great Britain in 2021 by Simon & Schuster UK Ltd

Text copyright © 2021 Danny Wallace
Illustrations copyright © 2021 Gemma Correll

1 3 5 7 9 10 8 6 4 2

Simon & Schuster UK Ltd
1st Floor, 222 Gray's Inn Road
London
WC1X 8HB

www.simonandschuster.co.uk
www.simonandschuster.com.au
www.simonandschuster.co.in

Simon & Schuster Australia, Sydney
Simon & Schuster India, New Delhi

A CIP catalogue record for this book is available from the British Library.

PB ISBN 978-1-4711-9688-1
eBook ISBN 978-1-4711-9687-4

Printed and bound by CPI Group (UK) Ltd, Croydon, CR0 4YY

This one's for Clover.
For making me laugh every
single day.

TO START WITH

Well, look, I don't know about you, but I found everything that happened EXTREMELY weird.

I think *everybody* found it extremely weird, if I'm honest.

Definitely me, and definitely Mum and Dad.

Sandra from next door definitely found it weird too.

The lady we met by the side of the road definitely

did, and so did Ernie, and I'm pretty sure Boring Paul must have.

Even the angry woman with the tattoos was probably just using all those bad words because she was coping with how properly mad it all was.

But, wait! I'm getting ahead of myself and I bet you're like, what on earth is this girl Stella talking about?! So let me start at the beginning. Let me start on . . .

CHAPTER ONE

So Sundays in my house are awesome because on Sundays we have Bobcroft Family Film Night.

Bobcroft Family Film Night is spectacular because Dad dims the lights and Mum makes popcorn, so already this is kind of a winner, right?

The whole of the Bobcroft family then strides into the living room.

My brother Teddy sits on the Big Chair in the corner

because he's the littlest.

I sit on the beanbag (which one day, when we finally get a dog, I will give to him or her with great pleasure because I love dogs).

And Mum and Dad sit on the sofa and make all those sounds like OOOH and AAAAH that grown-ups make when they sit down and want to tell you they're totally relaxing.

Dad picks up a remote and holds it in the air like he's about to start a race, to signal that Film Night is beginning.

And like LIGHTNING I pop on Mum's noise-

cancelling headphones and get my phone out.

Teddy gets his tablet out.

Mum and Dad press play.

And we all sit quietly and watch our films.

Mum and Dad watch their film on the Big TV. Usually it's one where people follow each other round an old house, saying long words at each other. Sometimes Mum and Dad randomly skip bits and I'm not sure why. I guess they're impatient.

I'll usually choose something exciting but age-appropriate and on Sunday it was *Dumbo*, which I was

greatly enjoying, though I have to say it was a little far-fetched.

So, just like every other Sunday, we're all sitting there, doing our separate things like a family, when suddenly it happens.

The music stops and the elephant disappears and now I can hear Dad again.

He says, '*Offle. Boffle woffle boffle.*'

So I take off Mum's headphones and now I can actually hear him properly and he's complaining that their film's just stopped.

He's sitting on the edge of the sofa and he keeps pressing the buttons on his remote control, but it doesn't help, so he presses them again but *muuuuch* harder, as if that's going to do anything.

Well, I looked at Mum and told her my film had gone too and she asked Teddy if his thing was still working, but it wasn't.

So we all just sat there for a bit.

And then we just put down our screens and went to bed.

Okay, I know that wasn't the most dramatic opening of all time, but you just wait because THIS is where things get weird!

When I woke up the next morning, all I could hear was panic from downstairs.

I checked my alarm clock but it was dead.

And even though I'd left my phone on charge just in case it came back to life in the night like a mobile zombie, that was dead too.

I could hear Dad in the kitchen complaining about sleeping in and being late for work.

He kept shouting, 'Alexa! What time is it?' and 'Alexa! What's going on?' and 'Alexa! What did I do? Why aren't you talking to me?!'

Mum was muttering something about how 'the systems' must have gone down, but apart from her and Dad I couldn't hear any of the other sounds I normally hear. I couldn't hear *Good Morning Britain* or Sky News on WAY too loud. Mum wasn't making her poached eggs in the microwave. *Zero* beep-beeps.

Dad hates being late. He says, when he was a kid, you

could never be late, because in those days you couldn't text people to let them know you were going to be late but you were on your way. He says if you were late, when you got there, everybody would have just gone somewhere else because you were late. And you had no idea where and you couldn't call them. So you just had to walk around for ages and hope you found them. What kind of system is that? Madness.

Someone should have invented phones a LOT earlier, though Dad says they had *one* in each house. Poor Dad, growing up like that. When you wanted to speak to someone, you had to phone their *home* phone and speak to a grown-up first! I mean, ex-squeeze me, but what? You had to talk to someone's mum and ask if you could speak to your friend! I'm sorry, but I have human rights. I don't need to get stuck answering boring adult questions about how Mum's getting on or how school is. Time is money.

Anyway, because of all the shouting, I go downstairs and immediately I can tell something is not right, right?

First up, what was that noise?

Answer: that noise was NOTHING.

There were no text-message DINGS.

There were no email WHOOSHES.

There were no bleeps or blips or tweety whistles or WhatsApp ting-tings.

Teddy was sitting miserably at the kitchen table with his blank tablet. Usually he'd be watching an age-appropriate video of giant airliners or something.

MISERABLE TEDDY →

BLANK TABLET

Dad's staring at his phone and shaking his head. Then he starts shouting about how come the toaster is working and the lights can turn on but the TV and his laptop are just blank screens? He says that's not how power cuts work. You either have power or you don't.

Then he says he's going to have to use the computers at work and Mum says she's going to have to borrow a laptop or something. Dad works up the road in Penzance, selling houses. Mum works from home, designing things for rich people who buy them on the internet. She doesn't charge very much. She gets very stressed though so she's got one of those apps she can stare at that tells her when to breathe. I think that's weird, cos I just seem to know when to breathe. I don't know why you need an app to tell you to breathe. Sometimes I creep up behind her and just shout *BREATHE!* This is not her favourite thing about me.

Anyway, just then there was a knock at the door and it was Sandra from next door.

She says have we heard?

And we're like, 'Heard what?'

And she says, 'Oh, you haven't heard then?'

And we're like, 'Heard what?'

And she says, 'Well, it's not good news.'

And we're like, 'Just TELL US what we HAVEN'T HEARD!'

Anyway, she says her telly broke last night and we're like, 'OURS TOO!'

And then Dad spotted Sandra was wearing a normal old-fashioned watch and asked her what time it was because nothing in the house was telling him any more. She said it was half past eight.

SANDRA FROM NEXT DOOR

Now Dad was double stressed because he knew he had an appointment somewhere at nine a.m. but didn't know what it was, or who it was with, because he keeps his work diary on his phone.

He walked out of the house, shaking his head, and got in his car.

And then he got out again because he'd forgotten his phone.

And then he got back in again because it wasn't like he needed it.

And then he got back out again because he should probably take it just in case he did.

Now it was just us, Mum was trying to pretend like it was just a weird blip or something that would sort itself out asap, but I knew that something seriously odd and WRONG had happened.

You might think I'd panic that all the screens and tech seemed to have just sort of vanished, but I am not a panicker and I am perfectly able to go without watching a viral video for a bit. Between you and me, sometimes I can't help feeling a little jealous or not quite good enough when I watch those things anyway.

Like, you know those YouTube or TikTok vids where

you click on one and it's some guy throwing a ball at a cat, and the cat hits the ball, and the ball bounces off a wall and lands in a cup? I've never done anything like that.

And I can't sing like this girl I saw on a foreign *X Factor* thing, and she was only eight.

And I can't do any of those make-up tutorials very well because Mum doesn't buy much make-up and what she does have is *for special*.

My old teacher used to say that not everybody can be

extraordinary, because if everybody was extraordinary, there wouldn't be any really extraordinary people, would there? Just extra ORDINARY ones.

Well, that's STUPID.

Because what I am really good at is being highly-organized. Which I know sounds a bit rubbish, but it is GOOD to be organized. I always know where my shoes are and no one ever has to yell 'Stellaaaa!' at me to brush my teeth. I take pride in always being one step ahead. The key used to be Post-it Notes, until I realized that was bad for the environment, so now I use the organizer on my mum's old phone. There's nothing more satisfying than a full calendar, complete with handy information. Like what time the chip shop opens and how many supermarket loyalty points I've got (five). I think I'm probably already the most organized girl in Mousehole.

I am also responsible. I award myself a certain amount of screen time each week, as recommended by the

World Health Organization. I enjoy order, planning, and knowing where I am supposed to be and when. I am regularly praised by grown-ups for my sensible approach, which is why I agree with my parents that now is not the right time for the family to get a dog because it would require more scheduling and planning. And even though I would volunteer to walk it myself every morning and evening and I could take it to the beach or run around in the woods with it, I agree that at the age of ten I am not old enough to do this yet.

And I am FINE with all this. I will wait for Jacinda.

Anyway, being organized is what I'm thinking about as I walk to school with Mum and Teddy because right now it's going to pay to be prepared. I can already see that this problem with the screens isn't just on our street. I reckon it's hit all of Mousehole.

The streets in Mousehole are steep and narrow and they wind round and round.

JACINDA

Everywhere I look, people are walking around with their phones out in front of them. Some of them look puzzled and some of them seem properly panicked. I'm getting a *major* 'watch out' vibe. Every now and again they'll tap at their screen, or press the buttons to see if anything starts working again, but none of them look happy.

It makes me want to check my own phone, but that's still blank too. Mum let me have her old one because she says, even though when she was young kids didn't have phones, it is better to be safe than sorry. Mum is always worried about me wandering off, or running into baddies wherever I turn, or maybe getting stuck in quicksand. I think she watches too much TV. I find a lot of adults have very vivid imaginations, but I think that should be encouraged.

Anyway, as we walk past the café, I look in the window and the TV isn't on like it normally is.

The nice thing is that people seem to be talking to each other. Even though all they're talking about is their phones. 'What is that, a Samsung?' I hear one man say to another man.

'It's a Sony,' he says.

'Has that gone too?'

'And my Kindle.'

'Weird, innit?'

'Weird.'

When I get to school, all my friends tell me it's happened in their houses too.

Charlie Fennel says they were watching *Dr Who* on catch-up and right when it got to the really important moment where Dr Who was going to save everybody, the telly just stopped. He said he was devastated because now he doesn't know how it ends. I wanted to be nice so I pretended I'd seen that episode and told him the way it ends is that Dr Who doesn't save everybody and actually just dies. Charlie looked a bit confused and sad, but at least he's got an ending now.

My teacher is Mrs Newington and she's new in town so we call her Mrs New in Town. She moved to Mousehole because none of the parents at her last school liked her. She used to work in London but she said she prefers it in Mousehole because people don't spit everywhere. It is a pretty good village so you should Google Earth it. It's got hundreds of reviews on the internet, and most of them four or five stars, so it's on point. And you can get a very big sausage roll at Hole Foods.

We've also got fresh air and lime-green water and crashing waves and little lanes. Oh, and two beaches! We don't go out that much though. I wish I could just go exploring on my own, but Mum says there's too many baddies about, even in Mousehole. We went out more when we were little. I used to love going into the woods and making dens. But, like Mum and Dad say, things just get busy, don't they? Grown-ups certainly seem to live in a high-pressure environment (at least that's what my dad says) and so it is only right we all make sacrifices, isn't it?

But I got a new scooter for Christmas and Teddy got a stunt kite when he turned four this year and we've only taken them out once or twice. I always imagine taking my future dog to the beach and letting it get all muddy. I won't care how muddy it gets, I'll always wash it. But right now we're allowed a bit of screen time before dinner, so that's okay too. I guess anything I really want to experience I can watch on YouTube.

MRS NEW IN TOWN

Anyway, Mrs New in Town told us her telly had broken as well, *and* her phone, *and* her smart watch. She usually does the register on an iPad but that wasn't working so she just wrote all our names down on a piece of paper, but then she didn't seem to really know what to do with it, so she just put the paper in a drawer and shut it.

She said we couldn't use our magic screen in class to learn today and that she'd put a DVD on for us about the history of the Post Office while all the teachers had an emergency meeting with the headteacher about what to do. But then, of course, when she went to turn the TV on, it wasn't working either. She seemed really freaked out about it all. I mean, if teachers don't know what's going on, then what are us kids supposed to do? Then she

21

tried to make us feel better by saying all the screen stuff was bad right now, but that the grown-ups would fix it soon. The government would be doing something. She said something about a cyber attack.

'What's a cyber attack?' asked Charlie Fennel and I told him that was how Dr Who got killed.

I thought all this was pretty fun at the time because it wasn't like it could go on for ever. We had a power cut at home once and it was great because we took out the board game me and Teddy got for Christmas and actually played it. And no one could cook because nothing worked so we went *out* for dinner.

I also didn't know what Mrs New in Town meant about attacks or the government. Why would they care about some TVs and phones in Mousehole? We're right the way down at the bottom of the country. We don't even have a McDonald's.

But Charlie Fennel said that his dad had been listening to the radio this morning on an old one he got out of his shed. He said that it wasn't just Mousehole that had been hit by this 'strange phenomenon' (cue spooky music). It was *everywhere*.

So Monday continues as normal, right? But while we were at school, learning about Ancient Greeks and their pots, it turns out all the grown-ups were more concerned about their phones and computers and things.

VERY IMPORTANT LEARNING

It's actually kind of hypocritical (this month's new word) when you think about it because they're always the ones going on about how it's kids that are going to get square eyes, and yet you turn their phones off for a bit and they all start crying in the street.

Dad is muttering and fiddling with an old radio when me and Teddy walk in after school. The radio's got paint all over it. I think a builder left it here when he did our bathroom. It's got a metal tube that you have to pull out from the top of it to get a signal and then you have to turn a button to tune it in. It's so old it looks like something Jesus probably used.

Anyway, Dad finds a radio station and there's a man saying people should phone in to talk about how they can't use their phones. It sounds like he hasn't had a single call all day.

Dad tries to find another station but when he fiddles with the button it's just static noise, so he gives up and turns it off. He starts talking to us about his bad day at work. 'The whole system is down,' he says, but I can't help thinking he's being dramatic. I mean, hello? Free day off! That's not exactly the worst thing ever!

Mum is being just as bad and panicky. She can't see if anyone has ordered anything from her website or not. She usually sends off a few packages a week of her fancy design stuff, but just lately she's also set up an eBay shop where she sometimes sells some of our old toys that we don't need any more. I wondered if it was for charity but Mum says it's for a rainy day.

Dad keeps checking his phone to see if it's working. It's like he can't stop looking even though he knows nothing has changed. Dad's *always* on his phone, but he doesn't use it as a phone. I know some people still use phones to actually ring up and talk to people – you see it on TV, don't you? – but Dad says that's the last thing he wants, to actually talk to people. He doesn't even like getting messages. 'Oh no!' he says when his phone pings with one. 'They want me to call them back! It's a nightmare!' And we all laugh at him.

Dad gets really stressed sometimes and I think he's a bit sad about his job. One night, after they'd had one of their arguments, Mum told me Dad feels like he's got to the ancient age of forty-two and suddenly thinks he should never have been an estate agent in the first place and that he's wasted his time. Last summer Dad bought a motorbike called *Blue Thunder,* which seemed to make him feel better, but two months later he had to sell it because sometimes we don't have quite enough money. The old man who bought *Blue Thunder* lives in Mousehole too, and Dad looks really sad every time we hear it zoom by. Once, when I was helping Dad in our front garden, we saw the old man roar by with a woman who must have been his daughter on the back and Dad just stood

there, staring. I've told Dad he could use my bike if he wants. Personally, I think Dad should be happy he is a forty-two-year-old estate agent. He could be a forty-*one*-year-old estate agent, with a whole year's less experience on the job! Plus he can take whatever he wants out of the stationery cupboard. (At my school the stationery cupboard is pretty empty. They keep asking the parents to provide the school with pencils and pens. Er, they've already provided the school with *children* – what more do they want?!)

Anyway, the doorbell rings and Sandra from next door comes in and says, 'Guess what?'

And we're like, 'What?'

And she says, 'No, go on, guess what?'

And we say, 'WHAT?'

And she's like, 'Guess!'

And we're like, 'Your telly's still not working?'

And she says, 'Yeah.'

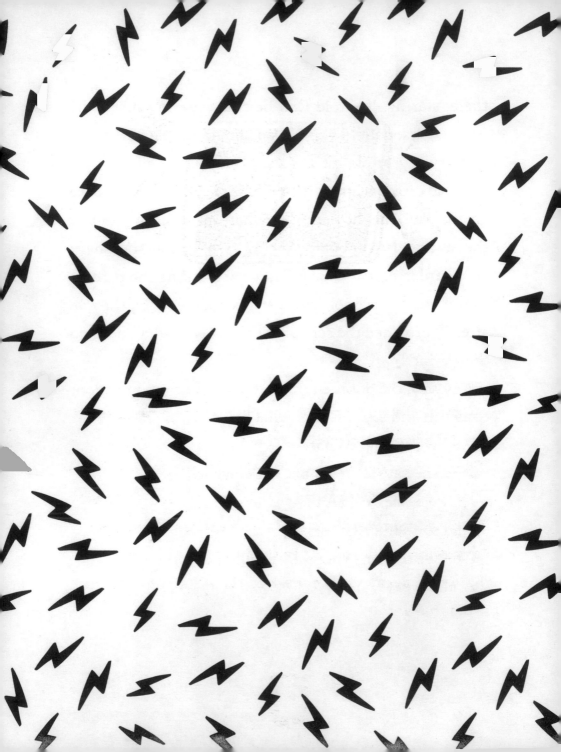

CHAPTER TWO

Tonight Mum and Dad don't feel like cooking because of all the weirdness and whatnot.

(*Total* excuse, but I'm good with it.)

Dad picks up the iPad so he can check what time the Chinese restaurant opens, and then he puts it down again and rolls his eyes when he remembers.

So we all decide just to walk to the restaurant and see for ourselves.

Mum and Dad still feel weird leaving the house without their phones so they take them anyway, even though you might as well just put a brick in your pocket. Mum brings an old comic instead of a tablet to keep Teddy occupied over dinner, but I don't need anything.

And then we step outside, totally without technology!

I ask Mum if we can go to the woods tomorrow after school and have an *adventure*, but she says we have to wait and see if there even *is* school tomorrow.

The idea of no school puts me in a very good mood.

The restaurant is packed when we get there. Everyone seems to have had the same idea. Mr Cheung is sweating, and he's had to put a sign up outside saying *CASH ONLY* because his card machine isn't working any more.

Dad sighs but luckily Mum has some money in her bag, so we can go in. I admire her for this. Mum is not a very practical woman but she often comes through in a crisis.

Some of the people who've come on their own are just sitting there, fidgeting, while they wait for their food because they've got nothing to do. Mum says that before smart phones people just used to read the back of peanut packets so they looked busy. I am not sure that can be true because it sounds absolutely . . . well . . . nuts.

One of Dad's friends, Ernie, is at a table near us. As we sit down, he says, 'What do you think's going on?' I'm not sure why Ernie thinks my dad will know, but not knowing never stops my dad from having a go. He will literally pretend he has an opinion on *anything*, which is actually very useful for his social-media numbers (he has twenty-four followers on Twitter: he used to have twenty-five but the newsagent unfollowed him after he complained about some M&Ms).

'Probably something to do with satellites,' says my

dad, and Ernie nods wisely.

'They're saying it'll all be fine by tomorrow afternoon,' says Ernie.

'Are they?' says Mum. 'Who's saying that?'

'The guys in the pub,' says Ernie.

Teddy keeps asking when he can watch planes again on YouTube. He can be a bit annoying sometimes because he seems to think this is Planet Teddy, not Planet Earth. Usually I would tell him not to just think of himself, but these are unusual times so I get the comic out and start to read it to him. But I'm still trying to listen to what's going on around me so I don't miss anything.

PLANET TEDDY

Ernie has given up sitting on his own and pulled a chair up to our table. He says that he heard on the radio that all the airports had to shut down last night because every screen in the departure lounges went blank and also none of the pilots could see where they were going, which I believe is important. He says that it's absolute chaos in London and all the hospitals are going mad. He says that even the traffic lights have stopped working because no one can control them with their computers any more. (I'm not that sad about that because it might mean that people start using their bikes more, which will be good for the environment and everything.) Ernie looks really worried by it all, but he also looks like he's enjoying telling us all this. He smells a bit of beer.

When we pay for our food, Mum goes to leave the change as a tip, but Dad picks it up and puts it in his pocket. He says we might need all the actual money we can get.

When we get home, Dad fiddles with the radio again and finds a station called the World Service. It seems like the really posh presenter guy must have been talking to Ernie because he says loads of the same stuff. He said at first people thought it was the billionaires who'd made the screens go funny, but the billionaires said it wasn't. They were like, 'We *love* screens!'

So then they'd said it must be some government somewhere, but that government was like, 'Are you kidding? What would we do THAT for?!'

Then the man said that everyone was really worried about the 'markets', which is ridiculous because I've been to markets and don't remember any screens. It's all just fruit and duvet covers.

Basically, I realized that NOT ONE GROWN-UP knew what was going on.

At first I was pleased it wasn't just happening in Mousehole (which would be *typical*), but then I started to worry because suddenly it felt really big and mysterious.

Anyway, Mum said we could have hot chocolate and we should read those books we never usually find the time to read, while her and Dad talked about grown-up stuff.

Teddy and I lay down together on his aeroplanes duvet and opened a comic. He was really tired and kept trying to use his fingers to zoom in on the pages. I stayed until he went to sleep.

Mum and Dad were still talking when I left Teddy. I went downstairs to see how long before they'd tuck me in. There was a woman on the radio saying it was really important we look after our elderly neighbours because old people might be feeling very lonely and anxious right now, especially those who live in the countryside and so on.

And that's when Dad went white and said, 'Oh God.'

I knew exactly what he was thinking because I was thinking it too.

It was the first time we'd thought about Grandma.

My grandma lives right on the other side of the country in a place called Rendlesham.

It's got a big forest and UFOs used to land there.

I didn't believe in UFOs until I saw a guy on YouTube who said they definitely exist and now I definitely believe they exist. But I don't believe what he said about them smelling like onions because that seems a bit odd. You get a lot of weird people saying a lot of weird things on YouTube. I saw a video once where a man with a ponytail was talking for ages about how the Earth is flat. But, if the Earth is flat, then wouldn't all the oceans just pour off into space? I don't think he was a particularly rigorous thinker ('rigorous' is last month's word and I love it). He even said that people all over the globe think the world isn't round. I mean, hello? What *shape* are *globes*? So I gave the video a rigorous downvote and Mum took the iPad off me because she said she needed to keep an eye on what I watch, which I very much agree with.

You won't believe what Grandma's house is like. It has

huge columns out the front like the White House and a big long garden filled with bunny rabbits and foxes, all getting along, like in a cartoon. There are trees and big bushes cut in the shape of cats. I remember it all vividly. I think Grandma's probably a secret baroness or an eccentric millionaire or something. I don't know what she is, except for a grandma. I guess even grandmas were something before they were grandmas? But I bet she at least knows the Queen. I bet they go bowling.

GRANDMA'S HOUSE!

SECRET BARONESS?

COLUMNS!

Dad's always saying to Grandma, 'We'll have to visit again soon, Mum,' but I've really only been to Grandma's once that I properly remember because it's so far away – it's eight hours to drive there, or ten if it's Dad that's driving, or twelve if it's Dad driving and there's traffic – and because things are always so busy. We went a lot when I was little, apparently, but now we use Skype instead. I remember going there when Teddy was born. He got most of the attention on that trip just because he had youth on his side. That's also why he thinks he can steal my chips or knock my stuff over whenever he likes. If they are not careful, Mum and Dad will raise a criminal.

Anyway, Dad gave Grandma an old computer she uses to send us messages and on Saturday mornings after swimming we Skype for a bit. Dad says that Skyping is the best solution for Grandma because it makes him feel less guilty. I don't understand why he feels guilty because I think Grandma must be delighted. She always seems happy, even at the end of our Skype calls, when

Dad has to quickly leave to reply to an email or Teddy starts to play Roblox or Minecraft or Mum drifts off to do her work stuff. I'm always the last one speaking to Grandma, so I get to end the call, which feels important. But now there's no Skype.

SKYPING GRANDMA

Mum seems really worried about Grandma, and I seem to catch some of that worry off her. Suddenly we all feel a bit helpless. Mum says Grandma's got no way of getting to the shops on her own and she will only shop using the supermarket delivery van, which she can't arrange without the computer. I had to give Dad a shocked look earlier because I overheard him joking that it would be the posh people who'd die out first because they'd be the ones standing at their windows, waiting for a van that would never arrive. Anyway, he says he'll phone Grandma in the morning.

'How?' says Mum.

Dad looks at his blank phone and says that's a good point. We don't have one you can plug into the wall any more cos Dad realized it was cheaper to use wi-fi.

Then he says he'll just ask to use Sandra from next

door's phone. She's still got an old one, just like she's got that old cooker and that TV that isn't flat. It's too late to go round now, he says, but he'll ask tomorrow.

But poor Grandma, all alone in that massive, creaky old house. With all those creepy suits of armour. What if she goes in the garden and gets lost in her own maze? She might be trapped there now!

I go to bed concerned that this is a very bad time indeed to be a grandma.

WORRYING

The next morning we all go into Sandra's and look at her phone.

Her phone is mad. It's got a big, thick curly wire, and it's green like a tortoise. Green! You have to put half of it up to your ear, and listen through a big round speaker. Also, to dial a number you have to put your finger in a slot and twist it round. It takes so long to dial someone's number you could probably walk round to their house quicker.

Anyway, to stop feeling helpless, we're trying to actually *do* something.

'Okay,' says Dad. 'Let's call Grandma.'

Mum sits down at the table with a cup of tea and says, 'Go for it.'

Dad stares at the phone, and then he stares at Mum.

'Right,' he says, 'so what's her number?'

'Oh,' says Mum, and she picks up her phone to find it, and then says, *'Tsk!'*

Grandma's number is stuck in Mum's phone and Mum doesn't know it off by heart. I get that. How could you be expected to know it off by heart? It's like twelve numbers or something. And Dad doesn't know it either. Usually you just go to G and press GRANDMA.

Mum once told me that when she was a kid, the way you kept all your phone numbers was to store them in your head. What a waste of brain space! You'd have an address book, she said, or maybe a thing on your fridge with all the phone numbers on, but you never took it anywhere. So if you were out you just had to remember everything.

HOW?

How could you store all those numbers in one noggin?

Oh, I'd better phone Paul: 9307896234!

Oh, I'd better phone Sam: 50 50 50 2 billion and 3!

And then you had to go and find a phone to actually do all that on!

Were people ROBOTS back then? Or was there just nothing to do except remember numbers? Half the phone calls people got back then must have been wrong numbers.

Then Sandra has an idea. She says there's that number you can ring to ask someone else to look up a number for you, sort of like a speaking internet. We crowd round the phone while Dad rings it.

A woman answers and Dad says, 'Hello, can you look up a number for me, please?'

And the woman says, 'I'm afraid that our screens aren't working so I can't look anything up. I don't really know what I'm doing here actually.'

'Oh,' says Dad.

And then the woman says, 'I don't suppose you know the number for a taxi?'

Dad did his best but it turned out the woman was in India and he's never even been.

So we can't phone Grandma and we can't text Grandma and we can't Skype Grandma and we can't email Grandma.

'We could wait for Grandma to ring us?' says Mum.

'But Grandma might not even know anything is wrong,' I say.

'Well, I guess we'll never speak to Grandma again,' Dad says. Mum gives him one of the Looks she uses when Dad does one of his jokes. But really he's just tense because he knows Grandma might be scared and waiting for him to call.

'What about writing her a letter?' says Mum, after thinking for a bit, but Sandra says her son Eric has a friend who says the Post Office is going to be shutting down from tomorrow while it works out how to do things without screens. This just makes us all the more worried about Grandma. What if she's just sitting there, on her big chair, staring at the door, all alone, without even a visit from the postie?

'Well,' says Dad, finally, 'I guess we're going to have to go there.'

'What about work?' says Mum.

'I can't do any work.'

'What about my work?'

'You can't do any work either.'

'What about school?' I say, and they both look at me.

This is all such great news.

They never cancel school! Even when it snows loads, my school seems to be the one school in the country where everyone is like, 'Keep calm and carry on!'

Turns out all that was needed was for the grown-ups to be affected by something!

Apart from not having to sit in boring lessons all day, there are three other reasons why this is great news.

First of all, I get to see Grandma.

Second of all, we get to save Grandma from feeling lonely and confused, which pretty much makes us superheroes.

And third of all – it's a family adventure! I don't remember us *ever* having one before. The closest we get is watching Dad play Zelda on the Nintendo.

Okay, so it's only sitting in the back of a car for ten hours on a motorway.

But it's a rescue trip, which makes it an adventure!

CHAPTER THREE

The next morning, Mum and Dad pack the car. It's not actually our car, it's Dad's work's car, but he got to choose the colour (red) and we use it all the time, not just when he's working. We have no idea how long we'll be away for, so we bring a bit of everything.

All Teddy wants is his iPad so he can watch *Paw Patrol* and I have to gently explain to him that we're going to look out of the window instead. He looks at me like

I'm mad. I tell him that we can pretend they're screens and won't that be fun? But he starts crying. Life will be easier when he's five and becomes a more mature travel companion.

I have packed all the essentials you need for an adventure, including a ruler, a compass and a protractor. Dad's bringing sleeping bags because Grandma won't be expecting visitors, and Mum says we can do a big shop for food and anything we've forgotten at one of the motorway services on the way.

I love motorway services. They're like little islands in the boring concrete sea. For some reason motorway services change the rules and laws in our family because I'm always allowed to play the arcade machines while Dad has a pee. I hope the arcade machines are still working. But if not, I will just have to come to terms with what Teddy will one day also understand: the fact that life can be cruel.

Dad says we need to drop by his office in Penzance to let everybody know he'll be away. Mum asks Sandra to water our plants, but says we should be back in a day or two. Sandra asks if we're going anywhere nice and Dad just rolls his eyes. I guess he's not looking forward to the drive.

When we get in the car, I make sure my pillow is nicely plumped up, and Dad starts the engine and says, 'Right!'

This is it! We're off!

And then we all just sit there for a moment as Dad realizes that the GPS screen in the car that tells him where to go is broken too. Dad has no idea how to get *anywhere* if the computer lady doesn't tell him. But he doesn't seem to want to accept she's not there at the moment, so keeps jabbing the button that says *Nav* and saying, 'Hello?'

Up until a few years ago, we didn't have any robot helpers. Now we've got loads of them, thank goodness. There's Siri and Alexa and the Google person and the lady who lives in the car and tells us where to go. I wonder how they're spending their time now the screens have gone. I hope they're all hanging out together, enjoying not being asked annoying questions like, 'What's the weather like?' all the time. It's beyond me how they don't just reply, 'You've got a window! Check the weather yourself!'

Mum decides that we're going to need a map and checks the little shelf on her side of the car, but there's no map in there, which she should know because there's never been a map in there. She laughs and says when she was a kid everyone always had a map in their car. A whole yellow book with every single road in Britain. Which, honestly, sounds like the dullest book ever!

Sometimes when Dad's work friend Boring Paul visits all he does is tell us how he drove to or from various places. 'Oh, I got the A9 until the B52 then the C3P0 was full so I stopped at the Burger King and had fries, a Whopper, some chilli-cheese bites and a Sprite.'

I don't know why grown-ups do this. There must be an age you get to where you think everybody needs to know how you ended up standing in front of them. It's not like I come down to breakfast and say, 'So I took the hallway to the stairs and then it was straight down and a quick right to the kitchen.'

Anyway, Mum says she can't remember the last time she even saw a paper map, and this doesn't help Dad, who's gone bright red and a bit sweaty.

'There'll be one at the office,' he says, and reverses the car out of the driveway, but because the screen that shows what's behind you isn't working, he immediately hits our bin. Then he gets redder and even more sweaty.

Luckily, Dad at least knows the way to his office because he goes there every single day. I think that means that deep down he must actually enjoy going there. Mum's brought the radio from the kitchen and extra batteries because she cleverly suspected the radio in the car wouldn't work properly. This is excellent organization on the part of Mum and deserves recognition.

There's also a screen in front of Dad that shows useless

things like how far he's been, but also useful things like how fast he's driving.

Anyway, that's all gone too. Did I tell you my dad was a slow driver? Well, guess how much slower he is when he doesn't have anything to tell him how fast he's going? Answer: REALLY SLOW!!

As we leave Mousehole, Dad seems to be doing breathing exercises to keep calm. It's a shame Mum's app isn't working because that would tell him how to breathe.

Teddy has already asked if we're nearly there yet about ten times, which I always thought was something grown-ups pretend that kids ask, but no, it turns out it's true. The first time he asks we aren't even off our street.

When we finally drive the few miles to Penzance, I start to notice something weird. There are big queues of people on the high street. They're all standing outside the banks and they don't look happy at all. What if it's because no one can do internet banking at the moment?

So they're having to crack open their piggy banks, and that's always a bit sad. Or maybe there's a sale on somewhere and they all need to get their money out pronto? I remember once at Claire's Accessories they did a sale on bangles and four people got arrested.

I notice a bit of shoving and pushing. And when Mum and Dad see the lines of people they give each other a Look and raise their eyebrows. I feel like there's something they're not telling me and suddenly this adventure makes me feel a bit worried in my tummy rather than excited.

Dad pulls up outside his office and runs into work. A few minutes later, he comes out again with a piece of paper he hands to Mum. Boring Paul waves us off from the window, smiling. He's told Dad exactly how to get to Rendlesham.

'A30, A303, M3, M25, A12, A1152,' reads Mum. 'Well, that seems simple enough.'

Everyone is being super quiet in the car.

We've been going about an hour and it's raining heavily and the novelty of this adventure is definitely wearing off. Teddy is bored and in a grump and is punishing us by not speaking. But he doesn't know that him being quiet is actually a bit of a reward, and no one wants to break the spell. So we just listen to the wipers squeaking and the raindrops battering the roof.

Dad is gripping the steering wheel tightly and staring straight in front of him. He can't relax because he doesn't want to make any mistakes. He hates not having the GPS. He says he's been scared of maps ever since he was a Boy Scout and he had to find his way out of the local forest using only a map. But it took him about six hours because he didn't realize someone had played a trick on him and swapped his map of Rendlesham for one of Russia.

Right now, we don't even have a map of Russia, but at least Mum has the piece of paper with the directions in her hand. You can tell she's bored because she suddenly starts making clicking noises with her cheeks. It's like having a dolphin in the car.

'Let's play a game!' she says.

We don't normally play games unless they're like

Words with Friends or Candy Crush or whatnot.

'You mean a real-life one?' I say.

Teddy immediately cheers up and says, 'Hide-and-seek?'

'That might be a little tricky in a car, Ted,' says Mum.

'Or a little *easy*,' says Dad.

'Can we play Tag then?' says Teddy.

But Dad doesn't want to play a game. He's become concerned because there's lots of traffic going the same way we are.

'Dad, can we stop at the park?' I say.

I've always wanted to go to Dartmoor National Park. I don't know if it's on the way, but it must be because when I've looked on Google I've noticed that it's on the way to everywhere. Mousehole is squashed right down in the bottom-left corner of the country, so if you want to go to Scotland? You go past Dartmoor National Park. You want to go to France? You go past Dartmoor National Park. I know nothing else about Dartmoor National Park except that every word in its name makes

FROWNING

it sound exciting.

'No,' says Dad. 'We're just going straight to Grandma's.'

I frown so he can *see* me frown in the mirror. So we're just going to sit here for hours and hours and not have a pee break or anything? Welcome to Broken Britain!

Dad seems really nervous and quiet. He gets worried every time he sees more cars joining our road because he doesn't have a screen to tell him how to get away from them. And every time the car makes a weird sound he gets jumpy because he doesn't know if there's something wrong with it or not.

'I mean, we'll have to stop *somewhere*,' says Mum. 'To eat our lunch and so on?'

Dad sighs.

'If we happen to go past it and it's the right time, then maybe.'

I look out of the window again. Maybe I don't usually

notice other cars because I'm watching something, but there seem to be a lot of broken-down cars stopped by the side of the road today. I've seen two red cars, a silver one and a black one. And each time the driver has just been standing outside in the rain, holding a broken phone, looking like they have absolutely no idea what to do.

Dad has gone even quieter, if that's possible. We've had to leave the main road and drive down a small country lane because there'd been an accident. He is not happy about it and is driving reeeeeaaaaallllly slowly.

There's no numbers I can look at to tell me, but I would estimate we are now going at 21.5 miles an hour, which has just increased our journey time by about 18.3 hours. That said, I have no idea what I'm talking about.

At least it's stopped raining, though now the lane is full of big puddles.

Dad keeps looking out for signs to tell him how to get back on to the road he needs, but instead all we see are signs for little places we don't need to go to. He seems annoyed that the roads are so narrow that you can only fit one car on them, and says he wants to get back to the big road, and are we nearly there yet?

I know where Teddy gets it from now!

'Oh great!' says Dad. A car is coming from the other direction and it stops right in front of us. It's a big black Range Rover carrying a big man in red braces. Dad has to drive the car on to the grass by a gate to let the bigger guy in the bigger car pass, and it doesn't make him happy.

'You don't want to head for the A30!' shouts the man from his window as he squeezes past.

BIG MAN

BIG CAR

I notice Teddy trying to hide his face in the corner of his child seat. He can be quite shy around strangers, whereas I find them interesting.

'Oh yeah?' says Dad. 'What's wrong with the A30?'

Dad always pretends he knows more about roads when he talks with other men.

'Tailbacks, mate. Both sides. Absolute 'mare.'

'Your screens working, mate?' says Dad, making his voice weirdly low, and the other man shakes his head.

'Stay at home if I were you, mate,' he goes. 'Turn the telly on and wait for it to come back.'

And then he roars off, way too quickly, scaring all the cows in the field next to us.

SCARED
COWS

'*Tsk.* "Turn the telly on",' says Dad. '*Then* what? Stare at nothing?'

'Okay, let's go,' says Mum, and Dad tries, but something's wrong.

The problem with driving on to the grass at the side of the road is that, with all the rain, the ground is now really, really soft.

The tyres on both sides have squidged into the mud, and the car won't go forward.

'Brilliant!' says Dad, unbuckling his seatbelt and opening the door, but I can tell he actually means the opposite. 'I'll have to push!'

Mum slides across to the driver's side and already this is exciting because Mum is a *very* different driver to Dad. She gets really aggressive and screams at people, which is why it's best if Dad drives. I have learned six of the seven bad words I know from driving to the shops with Mum.

She starts to rev the engine and Dad yells at her not to. He says she's only to step on the accelerator thing very gently when he starts to push. On NO ACCOUNT is she to do ANYTHING ELSE. She should NOT do it AGGRESSIVELY. She should do it the way a KITTEN would.

Mum rolls her eyes and Dad gets behind the car and tells her to, 'RELEASE THE HANDBRAKE!'

Mum does that and then IMMEDIATELY jams her foot down, which even I know was NOT what he said to do.

The back of the car slides about as the wheels spin madly and the whole thing revs like crazy.

From my seat I get a perfect view as Dad gets . . .
COVERED!
IN!
MUD!

When we look at him from the back window, I have to honestly say it looks like someone's made a bad statue of him out of chocolate.

Me and Mum and Teddy stay completely quiet.

I watch Dad slowly squelch to the side of the car.

He inspects the wheels.

He opens the front door and Mum quietly slides back into her seat.

We all look at him because he CAN'T be about to sit back down, can he?

But he sits down in his seat with a SQUISH, repositions the mirror, and says, 'On we go.'

CHAPTER FOUR

About one minute after Dad sat back down in the car, we start to realize that he didn't just get covered in mud.

We all have our hands over our mouths and noses because Dad stinks exactly like what comes out of cows.

It smells like a farm in here.

But we can all tell that it wouldn't be a good idea for anyone to point this out to Dad, who seems to be ignoring the smell.

'We could always stop at a hotel on the way,' says Mum, casually. 'Maybe have a shower, you know.'

'We are going straight to Grandma's,' says Dad. 'We are not stopping. Not for anything.'

Mum gives us a Look, then quietly lowers her window to let some air in.

Then she lowers my window and Teddy's too, and winks at us.

Dad is going pretty fast now, compared to how he usually

drives. The wind is whipping around, taking the smell with it, thank goodness.

But then the wind takes something else from the car . . . I look at Mum with horror as the small piece of paper with the directions on it suddenly flies out of her hand and is sucked out of the window.

She turns round and for a moment we just stare at each other with big wide eyes. I don't know whether to tell Dad.

She shakes her head at me and I shake my head at her.

But then we realize how annoyed he'll be if we don't know where we're going so we both suddenly scream, 'STOOOOOP THE CAAAAR!'

Since Dad hit the hedge, we can't turn the horn off. It keeps beeping on its own every few seconds, like an alarm.

Mum inspects the damage. The whole bonnet is hidden by leaves.

Dad is halfway down the road, looking in puddles. He has remained remarkably calm. Like, if he doesn't admit out loud that this happened, it hasn't happened.

'Was it about here?' he shouts to us.

'Further!' I yell back.

'Here?' he yells, a moment later.

I have no idea. I mean, it could be anywhere. It was a small piece of paper, and this is . . . well, it's the entire *countryside*!

Up ahead, a tractor is coming very fast down the road, bouncing along with a farmer on top.

'Ah!' shouts Dad. 'I'll ask the farmer!'

What's he going to ask him? 'Have you seen a minuscule scrap of paper with mad numbers on it?'

Dad stands to one side and raises his arm to stop the tractor.

'Excuse me!' shouts Dad, with a big friendly smile.

But the farmer's wearing ear defenders and doesn't even look at Dad.

SPLAAAAAAAAASH!

An entire puddle is thrown at my dad as the tractor speeds past him.

Dad stands there in disbelief, totally soaking wet.

Well, at least we won't have to spend any money on expensive hotel showers now.

'You all right there?' says the farmer to Mum as he spots the car and stops. 'Stuck?'

When Dad caught up, the farmer asked him if he'd swum here. It was a joke about him being wet. Dad had to pretend to find it funny but I could tell he wanted to shout, 'It was *you* that soaked me!'

Anyway, the farmer helped pull the car out of the hedge, then told Dad how to get back to the road we need. So that was fine, but then we realized the new problems.

1. Something has happened to one of the wheels and we're now slightly bouncing along, like we're driving over bumps all the time, even though we're not.
2. The car is still honking.
3. That puddle did nothing cos Dad is still *honking* too.

Everyone is just pretending things are completely normal, especially Dad, who is just grinning weirdly as the car goes *hooooonk* every three seconds.

As soon as he started the car, Dad put the heating and fans up to 100 per cent to try and dry himself off, but that kind of heat just makes the smell unbearable for the rest of us.

'Let's not worry,' he says, as we bounce in the beep-mobile, holding our noses. 'We'll be there in a little under ten hours.'

That's when I see Teddy is starting to look a bit car sick.

'Why does everything stink of STINK?' he wails.

'Do *not* be sick,' I tell him, sternly, and he nods at me and holds his mouth.

Mum keeps asking Dad if he's sure he knows the way. Mum explains to me and Teddy that before the Sat Nav lady and GPS you used to have to stop by the side of the road and ask a stranger directions.

And then when they started giving you those directions you would immediately stop listening. She said it was like a brain freeze. You would really want the information but the second you heard them you'd just start to ignore them. You'd just say, 'Oh thank you!' and go off in the vague direction they pointed towards in the full knowledge you had no idea what you were doing and then half an hour later just stop and ask someone else.

'I know which way I'm going,' Dad tells her, sternly, as the car becomes hotter than the sun.

So, half an hour later, we've stopped a total stranger by the side of the road.

Thankfully, the car isn't beeping any more, but now it's started making a sort of wheezing sound from the air vents, I suppose like beached whale might.

'Have you got the time?' asks the stranger, a grandma in a bobble hat. 'I don't know if I'm late or early.'

'No,' we all say.

'Do you know how to get to the A30?' asks Dad.

'You don't want to do that,' says the lady, suddenly noticing my dad is caked in dried mud. 'They're saying on the radio that everybody should stay at home. Essential travel only. So back home with you!'

'This is essential,' I tell her. 'We're rescuing my grandma.'

'Well, that does sound essential,' says the lady. 'Is she nearby?'

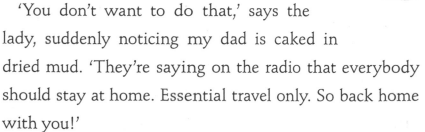

'She's in a mansion in a forest,' I say.

'Best place for her,' she says, and I wonder what she means by that. 'I'd stick to these smaller roads for now,' she tells Dad. 'Don't go through the cities. You know, I heard it's the new mobile-phone towers that did this screens business. They pump out shockwaves. Some people are saying it's alien technology.'

She winks at my dad and walks off. Dad gives Mum a confused look.

'Should we put the radio on?' I ask because that lady's made me a bit concerned.

'No,' says Dad.

'Well, maybe just for a second,' says Mum, and she switches it on and finds the World Service.

'Rising panic in London . . . fights outside betting shops . . .'

'How about we try and find some music instead?' says Mum with a smile, but Dad reaches over and switches it off.

Our car has started to rattle now, on top of the wheezing. I heard someone on a medical TV show once talk about something called a death rattle. I think that's what our car has. Like all the other disasters, Dad is completely ignoring it, but he is gripping the steering wheel so tightly it looks like he is trying to strangle it. I wonder if you can go to prison for strangling a car.

Mum is humming a happy tune and I know it's to try and cover the rattling.

I have no idea where we are but I am pretty sure it is nowhere near where we need to be.

'I'm hungry,' says Teddy. Dad grips the wheel even tighter.

I know he doesn't want to stop the car and I think it's because he's worried it won't start again.

'It *is* past lunchtime,' says Mum.

We didn't bring sandwiches because we were supposed to go to the service station as a treat, remember. Which means all we've had is a packet of cheese-and-onion Pom-Bears and a melted Twix.

'Do we really need food right now?' says Dad.

'I'm hungry!' shouts Teddy. 'I'm hungry! Hungry! *Hungry!*'

'He looks pale,' says Mum.

I get a bit jealous of Teddy sometimes. If I misbehave, I'm told to control my behaviour. If *he* misbehaves, there's always a *reason* to feel sorry for him, like he's 'tired' or 'hungry' or 'looks pale'.

'We wouldn't want him to be sick,' says Mum, doing a grimacey sort of face. 'That might only add to the . . . smell.'

'What smell?' asks Dad, and no one wants to say.

Then we all gasp because we spot an old pub called The Rose up ahead. It looks like a little old cottage, with pink flowers in baskets and a sign saying

This is an incredible piece of luck. Of all the places we could have ended up, we have ended up at the place with the best food in the country!

Of course, there is a chance they are lying. But that would be false advertising, and I'm pretty sure they would be in jail for that, alongside all the car stranglers.

'*Fine*,' says Dad, and the car rattles and thumps and bumps into the car park.

We sit at a table by the window and watch Dad outside as he opens the bonnet of the car. Even Teddy must know that Dad has no idea what he's doing. Normally, Dad would call a mechanic, or use Google to see what might be the problem, or maybe ask someone on Twitter. But now he has to rely on his own knowledge and, like I say, he doesn't have any.

He slowly closes the bonnet and walks sadly inside.

It's silent and empty in here, which seems weird to me considering it serves the best food in the country. There's a TV in the corner but they've put a black sheet over it, like it's died and they've done a funeral for it.

A lady with tattoos stomps over. Teddy holds a menu over his face because he still thinks that makes him invisible. The lady is wearing slippers and seems quite angry about everything. She says she couldn't print any *rude word* specials menu so she just wrote the specials on the *rude word* blackboard.

TEDDY (HIDING)

BEST FISH & CHIPS IN THE COUNTRY

BEST SPAGHETTI BOLOGNESE IN THE COUNTRY

BEST ICE CREAM IN THE COUNTRY

I see that today there's a choice between the best fish and chips in the country or the best spaghetti Bolognese in the country. For dessert you can have the best apple crumble in the country or the best ice cream in the country. I opt for the best spaghetti Bolognese in the country, and then if I'm allowed I think I'll have the best ice cream in the country.

'You know it's the environmentalists what broke the screens,' says the woman, like she's worked it all out and it's obvious.

'The environmentalists?' says Mum.

'Yeah. The Gretas and whatnots. It's all to do with liquid crystals. Once a screen cracks, the crystals escape and make the clouds disappear which means less rain so the world gets all hot. They're always moaning about it being too hot, that lot, but I say, what's wrong with a tan?'

She nods at us, all wise and that, but she is forgetting about global warming, not to mention skin damage. Mum gives me a Look which I know means I'm not to say anything to make the lady more cross.

Dad comes back from the toilets, thank goodness, where he has tried to wash all the mud and cow pats off his face and hands. He has not done a very good job. If anything, he has just smeared it around his face, like it's a dirty moisturizer. But at least the smell is less bad now. Now it's just like a light aftershave, maybe called *Eau de Cow*, or *Eau What's That?* or *Eau, Dad, You Stink!*

Dad points out to Mum what it says on the board below the menu.

NO CARDS.

'It's okay,' Mum whispers. 'We don't need the debit card. I brought the cheque book.'

She taps her head like she's a genius. I have no idea what a

86

cheque book is, but then Mum says it's a book full of forms that you fill out to promise you'll give someone some money at some point soon.

I mean, really? And people BELIEVE that? No wonder no one uses them any more because that seems like some risky business right there.

We wait for our food but then the lady comes out and says she can't do the best Bolognese in the country because she forgot the *rude word* microwave isn't working, on account of her not being able to tell what's on the screen. Dad asks if maybe she could cook it the normal way but she just makes a face like Dad has suggested she change the name of the pub to The Badger's a Butthead.

Teddy begins to slowly bang his head on the table. Normally, this would be a case for a child psychologist but I get it: he misses his normal routine. *Paw Patrol.* Roblox. Planes on YouTube. All of these things are better than waiting for some food from a tattooed woman in slippers in a weird pub.

I feel a bit sorry for him so I get a comic out and ask him if he wants to read with me. I start to do all the voices, and slowly he starts to forget that his screenless life is totally worthless.

While I'm doing that, Mum and Dad start to talk really quietly to each other because they think I'm distracted. But I can still hear them.

Dad is saying what if Grandma actually doesn't have enough food? She doesn't drive so she can't get to a supermarket and, even if she could, she might not have actual cash. They closed her local bank recently because people forget that some older people don't use banking websites, and she doesn't have friends nearby or neighbours. He says he's worried about the car, and some of the stuff that's going on in the cities sounds mad.

Mum says once we get on to the motorway we should be fine, let's not worry anybody (she looks at me and Teddy when she says this), let's just get there and hope Grandma's in a good mood.

Then *BANG*. A plate of fish and chips is dropped on the table. Without being rude, I have to say it doesn't look anything like how I imagined the best fish and chips in the country would look. I turn to Mum and Dad who are both smiling broadly at me, which is when I know stuff is really wrong.

'We don't accept cheques,' says the lady.

'Oh,' says Mum with a smile, looking at our empty plates. 'Oh dear!'

'It's the *rude word* banks,' says the lady. 'It's cash only.'

I think under the circumstances this is very sensible, but Dad looks infuriated. He nods to himself as he thinks.

'Okay,' he says. 'Cash only. Thanks.'

Mum makes an awkward face at him. But I know Dad will sort this out. Like Mum, he can be very effective in a crisis. I have to say that as parents they are very capable and generally set a good example.

'Could we get a round of ice cream?' asks Dad, smiling. See what I mean? The lady turns round to fetch it.

Mum nudges Dad like he's done something wrong.

'We don't have enough money for lunch, let alone ice cream,' she whispers.

'Kids, get your stuff together,' says Dad, quietly standing up.

Wait. What? What about the ice cream? What about the bill?

Mum's eyes widen as she realizes what Dad's saying.

'We're off. Now. While she's in the kitchen,' he says.

Now, we have not paid for the best fish and chips in the country, but I hear what Dad is saying, and I like it. We are now involved in an 'escapade' (thank you, word of the month for January). An escapade is like an adventure but not as adventurous. It's just exciting and can sometimes involve mild law-breaking.

'We can't just leave!' says Mum. 'We have to explain.'

'She'll make us do all the washing-up to pay for the food and we'll end up living here,' says Dad. 'She does not seem a very kind woman.'

'And I don't even think she was telling the truth about the fish and chips being the best in the country,' I add.

Mum and Dad suddenly remember I'm there.

'What are we teaching the kids if we do this?' says Mum and then she nods at the camera above the bar. '*And* we're on CCTV!'

'CCTV? The screens don't work!' says Dad. 'Now come on!'

We are making a run for it!

This is MADNESS!

We reach the car, Dad flings open the doors and I climb in and pull Teddy behind me. I put on his seatbelt and then do my own while Dad turns on the ignition.

Dad has never done anything like this before. He once had to go on a speed-awareness course because he got caught going too fast in his car and he was so ashamed he volunteered to set fire to his licence there and then, but the course instructor said it was fine and could he put the matches down. That's why he drives so slowly now.

I don't think the car is going to be good for a quick getaway though, cos instead of starting it just goes *WAW-WAW-WAW-WAWWWWW!*

'Come on!' yells Dad. 'Don't let me down now!'

But the car is stuttering and yawning and it won't wake up! So Dad says he'll push and Mum should get it going. He runs round the back and Mum takes his place in the driving seat and I keep looking out of the back window for the woman with the best ice cream in the country.

Then she's there. She's standing at our table, staring at where we'd been sitting, with a tray of ice-cream bowls in her hands and a confused look on her face.

And then she turns and we lock eyes!

'*Now!*' yells Dad, as Mum turns the key so hard it looks like she's trying to put the car in a headlock.

The car wheezes – then moves!

But.

We are moving at perhaps *four miles per hour*.

Dad is pushing the car as hard as he can. We are nearly out of the car park.

But really not very quickly.

The lady who was *in*side is now *out*side, literally walking alongside us, shouting VERY rude words at Dad. She caught us in about three seconds flat. It is

RUDE WORD!

incredibly awkward. I keep mouthing, 'I'm so sorry.'

Dad seems unwilling to look at her, I think because he is so ashamed of what we are doing and maybe because this is honestly the slowest getaway in history. It just goes on and on. You can hear the wheels slowly squeaking.

The lady has her hands on her hips and is yelling things like, 'What do you think you're doing?' and calling us 'thieves' and 'pirates'!

Now no one is looking at her and I start to worry that she might follow us all the way to Rendlesham.

And then the car finally finds its power!

'I'm so sorry!' yells a happy Dad as the engine comes to life. 'I'm so sorry!'

'You *rude word* *rude word* *very rude word*!' shouts the lady, and now I know a *new* rude word!

'I'll pay you back!' shouts Dad as he jumps into the passenger seat. 'I have to see my mother!'

And he slams shut the door and Mum jams her foot on the accelerator!

'Your driving is too aggressive!' says Dad, as Mum speeds down the road.

'Well, *I'm* driving now!' she yells, snapping her fingers right in front of his face.

The car is still very bumpy but Mum has taken full control, including turning down the heating so we don't feel like we're in the Sahara.

'Watch out for that car!' shouts Dad. He is a terrible passenger. He is very jittery and thinks everything is dangerous. Whenever he is in the passenger seat, he is always pressing his foot down like he's trying to find the brakes, even though he doesn't have any.

'That car is a quarter of a mile away,' says Mum.

Dad is right: Mum changes really quickly when she is behind the wheel. She is usually so polite and in control, but when we're in the car she turns the music up really loud and either acts really silly or starts shouting at old men she thinks are driving too slowly. Once she did that rude sign with her hand. You know the one.

Dad, on the other hand, becomes really serious when he drives.

Although, when I think about it, he has been quite serious for a while now, even when he's not driving.

As we speed away, I see all these vans at the side of the road, in a lay-by. Delivery vans. Brown ones and white ones and yellow ones. All the drivers are standing around with their hands on their hips. Two of them are playing football, but not with a football. They're using one of those plastic handheld screens they make people sign for stuff on.

'I'm BORED,' says Teddy. 'And I feel sick.'

'Slow down,' says Dad. 'If he throws up, those fish and chips will go to waste and we're not stopping again.'

'Which way is the A30?' I ask because that makes me feel very grown-up and also I feel it's important to get everything back on track.

'BORED!' says Teddy.

'Don't worry if they go to waste,' says Mum, turning

to Dad. 'It's not like we paid for them, you *criminal mastermind*!'

'I am going to pay that woman back,' says Dad. 'And keep your eyes on the road!'

'Lighten up,' says Mum. 'What else can go wrong?'

It's Teddy who sees it first.

'There's a police car!'

It's coming towards us very fast and its blue lights are flashing.

Dad gulps.

'I knew I shouldn't have let you drive,' he says, and Mum slaps his arm because it's not like it's her fault!

'Okay, are we all going to prison?' I ask. 'What do I pack?'

'Just act normal,' says Dad, as the siren wails louder.

98

'Just look like a normal family.'

'Our car is in bits and you're covered in cow pats,' says Mum.

But it's important we try, and so we all smile and wave as the police car gets nearer . . .

And zings *right past us*.

'He's probably going to The Rose,' says Mum. 'She'll tell him what car we're in and he'll turn round and get us because we were looting!'

'We were not looting!' says Dad. 'We were trying to pay by cheque!'

'BORED!' yells Teddy, which is MAD because we're almost literally in a Hollywood-style police pursuit, and we're getting away, fast.

CHAPTER FIVE

It's weird being in some random little village.

Dad reckoned we had to keep off the road for a bit. Lie low.

There aren't many people here. The ones I can see are just darting around nervously. I never would have thought that just losing some technology could have such an impact on people's behaviour. I mean, there are still parks, right? And people can still go out, or walk their dogs, or play with friends.

There's a small shop on the corner. A few people are walking out of it with big huge boxes of stuff. Toilet rolls piled up high on top of bags of frozen chips and bottles of water. Inside, I can see someone has just bought the last of the lettuce.

Me and Teddy find some squeaky swings on a small patch of grass, as Mum and Dad pace round the car, trying to work out what they should do.

'We need a map,' says Dad.

'The kids are bored,' says Mum. 'And you need a wash.'

I jump off my swing and give Teddy a few pushes on his. He wants to go higher, and higher, and he's absolutely loving it. He's properly laughing. I love it when he laughs because it makes me laugh too.

We used to go to the park more when we were younger. He'd toddle about and I'd pretend to be a dinosaur and we'd laugh and laugh together. Mum says Teddy would look at me like I was his hero. But then somehow it was winter and we stayed in and maybe we just got used to staying in and doing our separate things.

We've got a small garden round the back of our house,

and I remember when I was little it was muddy and overgrown and fun. Then we had the garden done and even though it looks much nicer, and I like the artificial grass and all that, it really hurts your knees if you skid along it.

But I feel like we laughed more before. In the jungle garden days. I hope I'm still an okay sister.

'Hey, Ted' I say, because I've spotted something. 'Come with me.'

Teddy has never been in a place like this.

The first thing he said when I pushed open the doors was, 'Huh?' Kind of confused, but kind of amazed.

I love these places. They say there used to be loads of them.

'This is a library, Ted,' I say. 'It's like a massive real-life Amazon.'

Teddy just looks at me like he has no idea what I'm

talking about.

'Imagine someone downloaded every book you could think of, printed them out, and put them all in here so you could read whatever you liked, for *free*.'

He starts laughing.

'I'm serious,' I say, leading him in. 'Like a Black Friday deal or something.'

It doesn't look like anyone else is here. All the computers have bits of paper stuck to them saying *Doesn't Work*. Then I see an old lady in a drifty long dress is behind a desk and she looks up at us, and raises her eyebrows.

'Hello,' she says, like she's shocked to see someone in a place that literally lets you do whatever you want for free.

Teddy looks equally shocked and tries to hide behind my legs, so I say hi to the lady, then quietly drag Teddy to the bit where I can see colourful seats because that must be the kids' section.

'Aw, *Millions*,' I say, picking up a book. 'Teddy, this is about two kids who find millions of pounds that's been thrown off a train and there's all this mad stuff about saints. And this one – this is called *Mutant Zombies Cursed My School Trip*. I don't know what that's about.'

But Teddy is more interested in trying to get the TV in

the corner to work.

I could spend a whole day in here. Mum and Dad would always read to me and rub my back before I went to sleep when I was younger, but then sometimes Dad would be late home from work or Mum was too tired or had to do her designs and they stopped doing it as much. Then when Teddy came along they started letting me watch something until it was time to tuck me in, which was fine by me, at first. Sometimes Dad still comes in late and sits with me. It's nice to see him there, on the seat in the corner of my room, his face lit gently as he scrolls.

I keep looking through the books and then I spot something I know will get Teddy's attention. 'Look,' I say to him. 'A book of aeroplanes!'

Now he's interested, and he comes and sits with me. We flick through all the pictures of aeroplanes.

'That one's an Airbus A380,' I say, like I know and haven't just read it at the bottom of the picture. 'And

wow – that's a Russian military jet.'

Teddy takes the book off me and, while he stares at the pictures, I rub his back.

He's really calm and I feel myself relax too.

The lady in the drifty dress comes over to us and I'm worried it's because we've done something wrong, but then she gives me a big smile.

'Have you found anything you like?' she asks.

'This is my brother – he loves planes,' I say. 'We're on a bit of a car journey and we don't have any screens, so I thought we'd pop in.'

She smiles, like people popping in is a nice surprise.

'I haven't seen you here before,' she says. 'Do you have a library card?'

Oh yeah. You have to be a member to borrow a book. I forgot that. In my head it was like having a giant Kindle or something and you could just take stuff. But I guess once you take a book out of a library, you've got the only copy they have.

See, that's another reason I like libraries. Most of the time, you get THE copy of the book. And you get to see its history, and who took it out and when, and you feel lucky because ONLY YOU have it now.

'Teddy, we'd better put that back,' I say, and then I smile at the lady. 'We don't live here. Sorry.'

And then the doors FLY OPEN and bang against the walls.

'STELLA! TEDDY?!'

ANGRY
DAD

'*Don't* walk away from us *ever* again,' says Dad, and I'm in proper trouble.

It's not that naughty trouble you get into, like when you won't eat breakfast or you've broken a thing they specifically told you they would prefer you not to break. It's that trouble when you've really panicked someone. It's *love* trouble, where they show you just how much they love you by making you feel like a really awful person.

'I'm sorry, I just got excited when I saw the library.'

'It's okay,' says Mum. 'But we don't have phones, and one second you were there and the next you weren't. Just tell us next time. There's no built-in app on a child. We can't press a button marked *Find My Kids.*'

I should feel really bad.

But just look at Teddy.

As we were leaving, the lady waited for Dad to stop telling us off before quietly sneaking me the aeroplanes book when he wasn't looking.

So now Teddy has *1000 Planes* and isn't bored any more, and none of us have to listen to him shouting, 'BORED!' all the time.

Dad is driving again instead of Mum. He keeps saying we shouldn't have stopped as all this stopping and starting will affect our fuel efficiency. The village clock shows it's after three in the afternoon, and I figure Dad is getting ratty because he usually has a Snickers Mini and a cup of coffee around now. At this rate, he says, we'll be driving 'till midnight.

After about half an hour of silence, Dad starts loudly complaining again that you just can't get a map any more. It's obvious that's all he's been thinking about.

'We should have got one at the library cos they had a *whole map section*!' I say. I'm just trying to be helpful, so I don't know why Dad immediately starts screaming and hitting the steering wheel.

I will never understand grown-ups.

Teddy is asleep in minutes, and I pull his jacket over his legs to keep him warm. Mum and Dad are mumbling to one another so that I can't hear. So I decide to just join in anyway.

'Can you tell me what's going on?' I say. 'Shouldn't we be listening to the news or something?'

Usually when there's a crisis they will have the news on all the time. It gets really boring. Not only do they have the news on, but then they'll listen to normal people ringing up radio stations, saying what they think about the news. I find that a little obsessive.

'We just don't want to put it on,' says Mum. 'We don't want you guys to get all worried.'

'Teddy's asleep,' I say. 'And I am unusually mature for my age.'

She laughs. Er, rude?

'Well, what does Dad think?' she says, and he waits

a moment, then shrugs.

So Mum turns the radio on.

Now, I'd always been under the impression that grown-ups thought too much screen time was bad. But it turns out that no screen time whatsoever is not much good either.

The news says that having no screens has been bringing out the worst in people. Because what if it just keeps going? Some people are realizing they're going to have trouble *making* money, and others are realizing they're going to have trouble *spending* money. Some people can't do their work already, and other people now have *too much* work. Everybody wants to know where the internet has gone. Everybody wants to know how they're supposed to run their business. The newspapers didn't come out today because no one's got anything to type on. Doctors can't find their records. People have started marching outside 10 Downing Street, and there's even been more crime. In some places, people have started stealing things, just because they know they can't be caught.

'Hey, Dad, that's like you!' I say, but he just gives me a Look.

People are worried about food shortages because everyone started using whatever cash they could find to spend on food just so they had it, but the supermarket ordering systems all went down and there's a delay because people have to work out how to use pens again, and the rail network is down, and *and and*—

Mum switches off the radio and turns to me. Evidently my eyes are the size of a giant squid's.

'Stels, it's important you know what's going on, but it's also really important you don't worry. It'll be okay. We'll get to Grandma's and everything will be okay.'

We zoom past another corner shop.

A sign outside says

A few hours later, it's that amazing time of day.

You know the time I mean? I think they call it Golden Hour. It's when the sun is nearly setting and everything looks all dreamy and warm. We get some great ones in Mousehole, where the whole harbour lights up and the boats all cast long shadows across the water. Every little ripple has its own reflection of the sun and blinks it at you; thousands and thousands of them shining, all saying hello at a slightly different moment.

Where we are right now there are mainly hedges. We've stopped in a small gravelly car park by some woods and the only thing that's spoiling Golden Hour is Dad kicking the front of the car.

He's saying, 'No,' a lot to himself.

'No,' he's going, as he kicks. 'No. No. No no *no*.'

Mum's trying to keep things light.

'There was a petrol station back that way,' she almost sings.

'That was miles away,' growls Dad. 'There must be one closer?'

The second the car started to run out of petrol Dad had gone into complete denial.

Even though the car was juddering and choking and jerking and jolting, Dad had just kept acting like everything was absolutely fine.

It was only when it had died completely and slowly rolled to a halt in the middle of the road that Dad had accepted we were stuck.

That was when he took his foot off the accelerator, pulled up the handbrake, and folded his arms.

I read on a leaflet at the doctor's once that when you get bad news, you go through all these stages before you

DENIAL

come to terms with it.

Denial. Dad had already been through this. That was when he was saying NO a lot out loud.

ANGER

Anger. That's where he'd just been. Kicking a car in a car park he'd had to push the car into.

Now it was *Bargaining*.

BARGAINING

'I think we can make this okay,' says Dad, nodding to himself madly. 'If we just push on, we can find a petrol station – we can do this!'

'Okay!' says Mum, brightly. 'I am sure there will be a petrol station just a little further on. And you can find it well before dark. And everything will be great!'

I've been telling Dad for ages he should get an electric car. One because it's better for the planet. And two because all you have to do to charge it is find someone who's got a toaster or something and then plug in the car instead. But Dad's work car is petrol, meaning you have to rely on someone on these tiny roads going: 'You know what this tiny road needs? A massive petrol station in case Stella's dad inexplicably drives down here one day!'

However, I don't think now is the time to remind Dad of my wisdom.

'Okay,' he says. 'Only take what you need. From here we walk!'

Poor Dad. He's only trying to do the right thing. For us. For my grandma. But everything that was normal has changed. Now it's like the world is playing tricks on him every time he turns round.

And then he actually turns round, and it's happened again.

He stares at Mum. 'What do you mean, "*You* can find it well before dark"?'

CHAPTER SIX

It makes sense that Dad went off on his own. We are in the middle of nowhere. I am a ten-year-old child, Teddy is only just four and we should not be forced to walk down random country roads at night in search of petrol. Plus I don't want to.

Instead, Mum has spread out our sleeping bags on the grass and found some snacks for us. Mum looks so beautiful in the evening sun. She's lying down on her sleeping bag, smiling up at the sky. Mum always seems a

bit happier than Dad, despite her shop not having many customers.

'Mum, how much longer will it take to get to Grandma's?' I ask.

'Oh, not too long,' she says, which using my parental translation device means AGES.

I already know it will take ages. That was just a starter question. Sometimes I ask a starter question before I get to my main question, which is the question I'm a bit scared of.

'Is it all going to be okay?'

Because you wouldn't think it would be that bad, losing all the screens, would you? You'd think it'd be fine, but then you think about how complicated and big the world is, and how everything is connected to something else, and it makes your head spin, and it can make your tummy feel heavy, and—

'Let's play!' says Mum. 'Let's pretend we're camping in the Wild West. And I'm a cowboy. But you're a robot sent from the future. And, Teddy, you're—'

'A dinosaur!'

'Perfect!' says Mum. 'You're a dinosaur sent from the past! And we've all decided to go camping together. Well, you know what we have to do first?'

'What?' I say, forgetting all our worries for a second.

The fire is still burning when I wake up. I *loved* making the fire. We'd collected so many sticks and dry leaves and old branches from the small woods around us. And we'd sung songs and even though Dad wasn't there it had felt normal again. The moon was high up in the sky and perfectly round.

It's a lot colder now though. So cold I can see my breath in the air. I look over and see Teddy asleep next to Mum who has her arm round him and she's sleeping too.

And then I hear a noise.

Suddenly I'm very aware of every inch of my skin. My tummy tightens and I hold my breath.

The noise had been a kind of *clunk-CLICK* somewhere out near the car.

I sit up and stare out into the darkness.

Wait. Where was Dad? Dad wasn't back.

'Mum,' I whisper. 'MUM.'

I hear slow footsteps on gravel and the snap of twigs. And now – someone was clearing their throat.

'MUM,' I whisper again. She stirs and blinks a few times, then she sees . . .

There's an old man walking towards us. He has a big beard, a weird old hat and a long coat. His eyes flicker in the light of the fire.

Mum draws us both close, as the man gets nearer,

stops, and says . . .

'You must be Mrs Bobcroft, is it?'

Mum screams! And I scream! And then Teddy pipes up and says, 'Are we nearly there yet?'

WHO IS HE?

'Don't worry!' says Dad, running over from the car and carrying an old petrol can. 'This is Uncle Tony!'

Uncle Tony is not our uncle.

Dad met him at the petrol station about five billion miles away. Tony had been dropping off some potatoes to his friend who manages the petrol station.

'So isn't that nice? Uncle Tony's going to help us,' says Dad, and Mum is all like pretending to be totally cool with it.

'Oh yes, that's nice,' she says, collecting our things up incredibly quickly but keeping me and Teddy well away from him because – you know – stranger danger.

'I only had the change from the Chinese meal to buy petrol with, and of course the screens on the pump weren't working, but Uncle Tony convinced his friend to give me a little anyway. Plus Uncle Tony said if we give him a lift back to his farm we can stay in his caravan and in the morning he'll give us a map.'

Dad looks slightly deranged. He seems so happy to have found some petrol, like things are finally going his way.

Tony doesn't seem bothered either way. He is maybe seventy years old. His coat has loads of holes in it. He smells slightly of diesel. There's a bit of straw in his straggly beard. He's got a

UNCLE TONY

WEIRD OLD HAT

STEELY BLUE EYES

BIG RED NOSE

SMELLS SLIGHTLY OF DIESEL?

HOLEY COAT

big red nose and steely blue eyes.

'Um, or we could just use the petrol and get as far as we can?' goes Mum.

But Dad says he's promised Uncle Tony a lift.

Mum said it might be best if she sat in the back with me and Teddy because it would be much more comfortable for Uncle Tony if he sat up front all alone with Dad and she was right at the back where she could be with her kids.

She seemed wide awake now.

'So, I don't think we need to stay in Uncle Tony's caravan,' she says, all lightly and politely. 'Probably best if we just drop you off, Tony, and then carry on.'

'You won't get far,' says Tony, quietly, and Mum does this gulp like from a cartoon.

'I could only buy a few pounds' worth of petrol,' says Dad. 'Uncle Tony says we can borrow some of his, from his farm.'

Teddy gives me a Look. I know what this Look means. It means: 'Why does Dad keep calling this man Uncle Tony and why are we going to his farm?'

'And I've got eggs,' says Tony. 'And the lil'uns might like to ride the bull in the morning.'

I don't want to ride a bull.

But Dad seems really into this Uncle Tony dude.

'Uncle Tony was stuck at the petrol station,' says Dad. 'I found him reading the farming magazines and eating a sausage. He'd usually have texted someone to come and pick him up, isn't that right, Tony? But you say you hadn't really heard about the global international worldwide screen failure.'

'No signal on the farm anyway,' says Uncle Tony, and Mum gulps again.

'Why are you called Uncle Tony?' I ask.

'Because I'm an uncle,' he says.

He doesn't say anything further but I guess he doesn't

have to. He's got a nice accent. I think it might be Irish. Or German. I'm not 100 per cent great with accents.

'So how far is it from here?' says Mum, sounding a bit nervous. I think she might be worried we are suddenly in a horror movie. She's always so worried about baddies that it's made me and Teddy worry everyone is a baddie too. Mind you, I don't blame her. It is so dark out here. There are no streetlights, and I can't see any signs. Just a single lane, and bushes that get higher and higher and higher.

'Not far now,' says Uncle Tony.

'So this is the caravan, is it?' says Dad, trying to sound happy, as Uncle Tony shines a weak torch at it. I think Dad's just relieved there's a plan.

The farm is called Angry Woods and it's extremely muddy. Every time I move my feet it's like the world is trying to suck my shoe.

EXTREMELY
MUDDY

Angry
Woods

The caravan has a sign on it which says *Bad Bertha's Resting Place*. I don't know if this is good or not but it doesn't seem good. The caravan is extremely small and very dirty on the outside. The only window has been boarded up with an old road sign and some nails. The door doesn't look like it locks properly and I can hear a cow or something shifting around nearby. I want to go inside, but at the same time I really don't want to go inside.

'There's no mod cons,' mutters Tony. 'No wi-fi. No TV.

But then there isn't anywhere now, is there? The world is quiet for once. None of that relentless babble. Life at last is silent.'

He looks up at the stars and breathes in, happy, then pounds his chest.

'FRESH AIR!' he shouts.

Mum looks terrified by all this.

'Anyway, it'll do for a night,' mutters Uncle Tony. 'I'll wake you up early for your eggs.'

Mum is finding whatever bits of old furniture she can to prop up against the door so no one can get in, but the problem is, the door opens outwards.

The caravan smells of old foxes or something, and there's a leak in the skylight.

It's cold. I can hear owls.

Me and Teddy are shivering in our sleeping bags on the saggy bed, pretending we can't hear Mum trying to keep her voice down.

She's like, 'What on *earth* were you thinking?!'

And Dad's like, 'We have hardly any petrol and he'll give us breakfast and a map!'

And she's like, 'He might be a *lunatic*! You let a lunatic called Uncle Tony into our car so we could drive to a farm called Angry Woods in the middle of nowhere at night so we could sleep in a stinking caravan called Bad Bertha's Resting Place! Who's Bertha? And is this where she *rests*? Or is this where she *died*?'

And Dad's like, 'We'll take turns sleeping!'

And Teddy sits up and says, 'Why do we have to take turns sleeping?'

And Mum and Dad say, 'No reason, darling!' at the exact same time in the exact same *everything is fine* voice.

They lie down beside us, propped up on thin pillows. Mum seems keen on keeping one eye on the door.

I go to sleep, listening to that massive animal or whatever it is outside, snuffling and shuffling about.

When we wake up, light is just starting to sneak in through the skylight. The first thing I notice after that is the smell. But the second thing I notice is that the whole caravan is moving from side to side.

It's properly shunting from left to right. Like a seesaw. The whole caravan!

'Wake up!' says Mum. 'WAKE UP!'

Dad has obviously been dreaming and screams, *'I will PAY for the food, madam!'*

We all sit up in bed.

And we cannot quite believe what we are looking at.

It's in front of us, standing at the edge of our bed, looking VERY confused indeed.

'A COW!' yells Dad.

He's right. A cow. Just there. A cow at the end of our bed. A cow right here in this caravan.

'Get it out!' screams Mum.

'How?!' shouts Dad.

'I don't know!' screams Mum.

'Why is that a cow?' asks Teddy.

The cow has massive eyes and enormous nostrils and it doesn't seem happy we're here. It's got mud all over its ankles and, dare I say it, a very bad attitude.

Dad begins to try and give it a speech.

'So, cow, here's the thing—'

The cow suddenly sneezes in Dad's face.

'I've been SLIMED!' he wails, blinded by whatever bright-yellow badness just shot out at him.

'Cow! Out!' says Mum, in her best Mum voice.

Then she kneels on the bed and puts one hand on her hip and points at its face.

'Bad cow!' she says.

It has no effect.

'BERTHA!' comes a voice, and then Uncle Tony rocks

into the caravan, carrying a massive shotgun.

Mum and Dad scream but I don't know what they're worried about. The cow seems the most pressing matter. We can deal with the mad gunman after.

'This is where Bertha sleeps, normally,' says Uncle Tony, who I notice is wearing exactly the same clothes as last night. 'I told you, Bertha – we have guests! You have to use the lower field, like the other cows.'

He looks at us to explain, still waving his shotgun about.

'She treats this place like a B&B,' he says. 'Thinks she's my wife!'

None of this makes Uncle Tony sound more normal.

'What time is it?' I ask.

'Breakfast time,' he says. 'Five thirty a.m.'

Okay, so let's be clear: that is so *not* breakfast time.

Dad blinks and wipes his mouth.

'Uncle Tony,' he says, politely. 'Is there anywhere I can wash this excess cow gunk off my face?'

'Use the tap by the pigs. After that, we get to work.'

We all stare at him.

What does he mean, 'work'?

CHAPTER SEVEN

I felt sorry for Mum. She'd never milked a cow before, and it didn't look like she'd turn semi-pro anytime soon.

She looked horrified when we first saw her sitting on that stool near the pond; she couldn't even look at the cow. She just had to keep squeezing its udders, which she said felt too personal. And the milk was going everywhere except the orange bucket. She had milk on her shoes and milk on her trousers, and I don't know if I told you, but she's generally dairy intolerant. Every time she squeezed an udder she made a little 'ew' sound.

Ew squirt ew squirt ew squirt.

I'm sure that once upon a time that would have made Dad laugh, but he wasn't in a particularly jolly mood right now.

He'd been told to clean out the pig houses.

They don't really look much like houses to me. They look more like pigloos.

Dad was doing his best, although he wasn't really wearing the right clothes. He was still wearing what he'd been wearing yesterday, which was essentially what he'd been wearing to the office, except with cow pats on. Now he had a shovel, a brush and a scraper and he was removing everything from the floor that had once been in a pig. He kept making that weird face grown-ups make when they're really disgusted by something. He kept jerking his

PIG POO!
↓

head back and forward like a chicken and sticking his tongue out because whatever he was doing was turning his stomach. Meanwhile, pigs kept nudging at his legs and grunting. A particularly big one with a bush of black hair seemed to have a real problem with him. I think he saw straight through my dad's bravado.

VERY
BIG PIG

But me and Teddy? We're fine. Our job is to collect the eggs from the chickens, and each of the chickens has a different name.

'That's Laura,' says Uncle Tony, walking alongside us. 'That's Samantha. And that one over there is Egbert.'

'Haha!' I say. 'Egbert because it sounds like "eggs"!'

'Eh?' says Uncle Tony, and I decide not to press it any further. Also, I thought chickens were all girls. I would not want to be a girl called Egbert. Things are hard enough.

Collecting eggs is not as easy as it sounds though. You have to be gentle with the chickens. You have to smile at them, and apologize, but still be rather firm. And you have to do it quickly. You lift up the hen, say, 'Thank you for the eggs,' pop them in the basket and move on before they ask too many questions.

'So what's your story then?' says Tony. 'What do you kids do?'

I thought he meant for a living, so I say, 'I'm currently

143

unemployed, unless you count professional schoolgirl.'

'For fun I mean. What makes you laugh? Knock Down Ginger? Marbles?'

Marbles? What year did he think this was? And Knock Down Ginger is where you knock on people's doors and run away. Also known as Ding Dong Ditch. I'm pretty sure people are jailed for that.

'Well, Teddy likes aeroplanes and no, I don't really like marbles.'

'What kids don't like marbles?' he replies.

'Marbles are a bit chaotic,' I say. 'I find it stressful that they just go everywhere. I prefer more controlled world-building like in Roblox or Minecraft and so on.'

'Don't sound like you get out much.'

I smile because, although this is meant as an insult, he's right. It's nice to be out here. Doing something. Fetching eggs with a breeze on my face. Being kind to chickens. There are literally zero chickens in my house.

'You're a natural farmhand,' Uncle Tony says. 'But you

don't get it from your dad.'

I look up and see Dad is slipping around in all the muck and mud, using his shovel to try and keep his balance, like one of those gondoliers you see on *Newsround* when they do a thing about Italy. That big

pig didn't like what Dad was doing at all.

'How old are you?' says Teddy, suddenly.

I know it might not seem like much to you, but this was quite brave for Teddy. I was proud of him.

'How old am I?' says Uncle Tony. 'How old do you think I am?'

Teddy stares at him, then says, 'Fifteen?'

'I'll be eighty next month,' says Uncle Tony.

'Are you having a party?' says Teddy.

'No,' says Uncle Tony.

I feel a bit sorry for Uncle Tony then. I mean, everyone should have a party with their friends on their birthday. Although I don't even know what you'd do for an eightieth birthday party. You probably don't go to a trampoline park or whatever.

'What do you do with all these eggs?' I ask.

'Pop 'em in boxes,' he says. 'Along with a cauliflower, a few potatoes, some carrots and onions. Bottle of milk. Maybe some flowers from the meadow if I've time.'

'And then what?'

'Drop 'em round the old folks' houses,' he says. 'Them that can't get it for themselves.'

'Don't you sell any of it?'

That's when Uncle Tony shakes his head and looks off into the distance, like how they do in films. A bit melancholy (word of the month in February).

'I've got fields full of food, but farm's coming to an end, I think,' he says. 'My knees are shot. There's no one around to help pick the veg any more or sort out the chickens or the cows. People want it all online anyway, not from little farms like mine. They get it all from the supermarkets with their vans. So best I just give this stuff to people who need it. Problem is, there's so much of it and it'll be wasted.'

Just then there was an almighty YELL. Dad was running away from that massive pig. Dad had opened up the gate to the pig houses and it had seen its chance.

Dad was headed straight for the pond, screaming and yelling, with a giant thundering pig squealing right behind him.

We all just sort of ignored it.

'Your dad said you're on your way to see your gran,' says Uncle Tony.

'We don't see her much and with all this going on we thought we'd better . . . see her,' I explain.

'You ever wonder why you don't see her much?' he says, like he knows something.

I frown at him because how can he know more than me about my family?

'Well,' I say, 'she lives miles away. And my mum and

dad are busy with work. And we have Skype so it's fine.'

'Then it's fine,' says Uncle Tony, but something about the way he says it makes me think he doesn't really think that at all.

'So, Uncle Tony,' says Dad, shivering, as we stand outside our car. 'Is there any chance I could have a quick shower before we head off?'

Dad still has bits of old reeds and pond dirt in his hair. I bet if you checked his pockets you'd find a fish in one of them.

'Shower?' says Tony. 'Don't have one. Don't believe in them. What's wrong with you? You just had a swim in the pond!'

He makes it sound like Dad had a choice.

'Here's your petrol,' says Tony, handing over a big red canister. 'Don't have much but it should get you most of the way there.'

Then he points at a box he's already laid on the bonnet of the car. 'And some milk and vegetables for when you get there.'

'Thanks for letting us stay, Uncle Tony,' says Mum.

'One more thing,' says Uncle Tony. 'Your map.'

Dad looks delighted he's going to get a map at last. But his face falls when he sees what Uncle Tony is holding out to him.

'Did you not have a proper map?' says Dad.

'What's wrong with this one?' says Uncle Tony, frowning. 'I drew it myself.'

Dad looks at the scrappy paper and the thin lines drawn in biro.

'It's got "Here Be Dragons" written on it as we approach the A12.'

'Kept it exciting,' says Uncle Tony with a wink. 'For the lil'uns.'

It was sad to say goodbye to Uncle Tony. I felt like he'd kept us safe for a bit and I liked being around all the animals.

I had the cardboard box of vegetables on my lap as Dad waved him goodbye and pulled away from the farm.

'Well, that could have been worse,' says Mum, looking relieved. 'He could have had *two* shotguns, *two* sneezy cows and *two* angry pigs.'

Then she squeezes Dad's hand.

'I think you secretly enjoyed bits of that though. Am I right?' she says.

What's she on about? Why would she think Dad enjoyed waking up to a cow and being chased by a pig?

But I can see Dad trying not to smile.

'Something about it,' he says. 'Just being somewhere else. Doing something new.'

I just keep quiet and watch because it feels like they're properly agreeing on something, though I don't quite get what.

'Feels like there's a lot more going on when you look around, doesn't there, kids?' says Mum. 'I want to get to Grandma's and *make* things. Grow things. Play things. See things. So step on it, Dad!'

'I refuse to drive aggressively,' replies Dad. 'It's lunchtime on a new day. We'll be there early evening. Let's just not stress. I am fed up of being stressed. I thought I was stressed at work. I thought I was stressed in life. But here I am with no work stress and a totally different life and also every time I'm stressed I end up filthy or in a pond.'

Dad always thinks he can fix things, but it seems like without all his tools – his phone, his computer, his email, his texts – he's realized it was just him and Mum and us and maybe we should just let whatever happens happen.

I'm starting to think he's right. As you know, I pride myself on being organized. But, if all you worry about is doing the right thing at the exact right time, maybe that means more can go wrong. I used to think that being spontaneous was all well and good, so long as you planned it properly. But watching Dad up close has made me think perhaps it's okay to let go.

Mum and Dad have gone a bit quiet and I decide I should just do what I feel, and ask the thing that's been on my mind since this morning.

'Dad, Uncle Tony was asking about Grandma and why we don't see her more than we do,' I say.

He looks at me in the mirror.

'Oh, uh, yeah,' says Dad. 'Basically, Tony had a fight with his sons years ago about the farm. He was telling me on the very, very, *very* long walk back to the car last night.'

'What kind of fight?' I say.

'A disagreement, that's all,' says Dad. 'These things

can happen. It's very complicated. And now they don't really see each other much.'

I wonder if that's why he calls himself Uncle Tony. He must have a nephew or a niece somewhere who called him that. Maybe he's hanging on to it. There are some things that even if they're taken away you can still keep hold of.

So, anyway, this makes me look at his vegetables for some reason. Don't ask me why. Maybe because it was the only thing I had of his. I don't just immediately look at vegetables when I'm sad. It's not like every time I stub my toe I immediately yell, 'Bring me a courgette! I must stare at it to end my pain!'

There are some baby potatoes, which are cuter than normal potatoes. There's some rosemary (I think?) and there's carrots.

But I notice something in between the potatoes and the carrots. A small bag with a drawstring.

ROSEMARY?

BABY POTATOES (CUTE!)

CARROTS (NOT SO CUTE)

I pull it out and pour what's in it into my hands. Marbles!

They click and clack together and make that squeaky sound that makes your teeth feel funny. I hold one up to the sunshine. Such a small thing, but it's like there's a whole different universe to be found in there if you just take the time to look.

And there's something else in the bag. A polished metal badge, almost like a medal, with a picture of a

plane on it, and underneath, in blue, the words *Royal Air Force*.

I nudge Teddy and hand it to him.

'Cooool,' he says.

'That's from Uncle Tony,' I say. 'To make you happy.'

Dad slows down as we come up behind a bunch of cyclists who are taking over the whole road. I look at Dad because I know he hates cyclists. Maybe he never had a bike when he was a kid. Sometimes I wonder if he ever played at all. In Mousehole, when he has to get to Penzance in a hurry, he'll always end up stuck behind some cyclists on a road and be fuming. I see Mum glance at Dad to see if he's going to kick off. But this time Dad just takes a deep gulp of air, leans back in his seat and drives more slowly.

'Shall we put the radio on?' says Mum.

'Music,' says Dad. 'Just some music. No news.'

So Mum puts on the radio and finds some music.

Normally, if we go on a long drive, I would organize a complete playlist, with a range of options for every mood. And I'd have listened to it quietly on my headphones, while Mum and Dad put something random on the radio. I always thought that was the weird thing about radio. Like, when you listen to the radio you can't even choose what song to hear. You can't press a button and immediately get what you want. With radio, you get what you're given. Things you've never heard before. Which seemed much too disorganized for my liking.

But actually I suppose there are more surprises that way. Like on this trip.

'When I was a kid, you used to have to record the songs you wanted to hear off the radio,' Dad says to us, looking all daydreamy.

'Record them?' I say.

'You used to have to get a tape and stick it in a cassette player and then press play and record at the same time when the song you wanted came on. So you'd always miss the beginning and there'd always be some random DJ talking over the start of it.'

It's nice that Dad is sharing but I have literally zero idea what he's going on about. Why would some random DJ start talking over your favourite songs?

'I used to record my own radio shows,' says Dad. 'All my favourite music, with me in the middle saying things like, "The weather today is tremendous!"'

Then a song comes on the radio that Mum loves. It's got a man saying mad stuff. Honestly, like bizarre stuff, like *'You're twistin' my melon, man!'* and somehow Mum knows all the ridiculous words, which is just cringe. And now Dad is smiling, and he's raising his arms, and the two of them now start singing about twisting melons, which is just about the worst thing I have ever been through in my life. Even Teddy looks embarrassed.

But then they look at each other and it's like it's just the two of them and this time Dad squeezes Mum's hand. And the moment is only spoiled about five seconds later.

'How hard can it be to change a tyre?' says Mum, opening up the boot and realizing that she's going to have to take all our stuff out before she can find the spare one.

We're in a small lay-by and Dad's leaning on the bonnet of the car, staring at Uncle Tony's map. It's quite a complicated-looking map, full of unusual notes and strange doodles. There were some rules he'd put at the bottom, including: AVOID BIG ROADS, DON'T GO DOWN NOTHING WITH AN 'A' IN THE TITLE and THERE'S A CRACKING PORK BREAKFAST AT THIS CAFÉ.

Dad wasn't exactly sure where we were. We could see the names of places on small road signs, but without anything to check them against we might as well have been in space. Still, the sun was shining, the radio was working, and Mum reckoned changing a tyre was easy. Or it better be because it wasn't like we could look up a number or call anyone. But Mum said she used to have to do it all the time when she got her first car back in 1890 or whenever it was.

'Right!' she says, pulling out the spare from a secret hidden compartment I had no idea was there. That's like a magic trick in itself.

This is the first time I've seen Mum holding a tyre.

It's funny when you find out your parents can do special things, or have hidden skills. Charlie Fennel's mum calls herself an 'experimental hairdresser', but she's not allowed to do it any more because of a court case.

HIDDEN SKILLS!

Mum gets this thing called a jack out, slides it under the car, and starts to crank it. The car immediately gets higher! How does she know how to do this? Is there some Mum School or something?

'Stand back, Teddy,' I say, as Mum moves on to part two: undoing the bad wheel.

'Right, lug wrench,' she says, holding her hand out and looking at Dad, expectantly.

'I beg your pardon?' he says.

'Do you have the lug wrench? For the wheel nuts? Because it's not in there.'

'You think I just walk around with a lug wrench? I don't even know what a lug wrench is!' says Dad.

Mum looks at me and Teddy, and we just shrug because why on earth would we have a lug wrench?

'Right,' says Mum.

Then I hear something. A slow, growling, engine-like noise.

It gets louder and we all stop what we're doing.

Teddy takes a step back in case it's one of Uncle Tony's dragons or whatever.

And around the corner it comes: a massive, hulking, fuming truck.

A thing like that shouldn't be on a road like this.

But down the road it squeezes, like a giant rat somehow getting through a drainpipe. Its huge wing mirrors brush against the trees and bushes.

As it gets closer to us, it blocks out the whole sun.

And then it stops.

And a window slides down.

I get the feeling whoever this is will be helpful. Maybe they'll be able to fix our tyre. Or maybe they'll be able to tell us the quickest way to Grandma's!

Then this man leans out and goes, 'Don't suppose you know where we are, do you, cos I am proper lost!'

CHAPTER EIGHT

Dad is sharing Uncle Tony's map with Trucker Terry, and they both look confused.

'Why does it say there are dragons on the A12?' he asks, and Dad tells him not to worry about it.

Terry tells us the government have said people are only allowed to do local journeys right now. That sucks for us because we are definitely not local. Terry says they've shut the motorways because they're worried about not spotting accidents on the broken CCTV and to keep people in their homes. Apparently, there were supposed to be big demonstrations in Birmingham and Glasgow today called 'Scream 4 Screens', but no one could find out the right information about where to meet and scream so they all went home again. That's what Terry says anyway.

Meanwhile, Mum has borrowed a lug wrench off Terry and is busily swapping the wheel over while Teddy pretends he's helping by handing her small pieces of gravel or leaves.

I really want to take a picture of Mum being awesome right now, but of course I can't. Apparently, before you could take photos on your phone or your tablet or your memory card or whatever, you had to go to an actual shop to have your pictures printed out for you. And you only printed out like twenty of them. And you didn't even get to see them before you printed them. And the shop would take about a week to get round to it. I think that's why there aren't that many pictures of my parents as kids. You had to really decide which moments were worth photographing. I guess people just tried to remember stuff more. So I will just try and remember this moment.

I blink hard, like a camera shutter.

Also, while I'm on the subject, there's like zero videos of my parents as kids. It's like they didn't start to exist until they were about twenty. That's mad, right? All I have to do is eat a cupcake or kick a ball and it's like my parents think they're a TV news crew. Every single Christmas concert at school I've ever done is recorded for the full two hours in high resolution, which is great, but also like the last thing anyone wants to watch ever again in their lives. But, if a thing isn't recorded, how do you know it even took place? I mean, if you can't remember watching it through a screen, did it ever happen? I think that's what I took for granted just now, until I blinked at my mum, and made a memory.

It's hard to imagine my dad as a kid. It's hard to imagine him not worried, or not in a tie, or not sitting at a desk, staring.

'Oh, wait!' says Trucker Terry, suddenly, and then he turns the map on to its side and both him and Dad, 'Ohhhhh!' and seem to understand it better now.

'There!' says Mum, wiping the sweat off her forehead. 'All done. So where are you headed, Terry?'

'Oh,' says Terry. 'Well, staying local. Avoiding London and the cities because of all the . . .'

He looks at me and Teddy.

'Because of all the *obvious* reasons,' he says. 'You know, they're saying it's the tech firms what done this. This screens business.'

'The tech firms?' says Dad.

'Well, they make so many screens, don't they?' says Terry. 'Rumour is they wanted all our screens to break so they could make loads of new ones for everyone to buy. Anyway, I was supposed to be volunteering, delivering a whole load of fruit and veg to the charities and foodbanks and so on. But the supermarkets got their orders all wrong and then there was the panic buying, so in the end there was nothing to pick up or deliver.'

'Wait,' I say. 'So some people can't get food?'

'It's the ones without much money,' says Terry. 'People

got in a panic and cleared the shelves. Especially in the little villages. Anyone who's selling any food is realizing they can sell it for more money! Everyone turns into pirates in a crisis, don't they?'

'My daddy made us leave a restaurant without paying,' says Teddy.

'But you can't get any food to people?' I say, and Terry says no. He says normally he'd just go home and watch TV or something, but he can't even do that.

Mum and Dad start to talk to Terry about how awful it is that we live in a world that could even need foodbanks and that no one should have to rely on one, but I don't feel like just talking about it is doing anything so I decide to speak up with an idea.

'Have you heard of Angry Woods Farm?' I say.

'No,' says Terry.

So I take the map and show him where our route began.

'It's there,' I say. 'Uncle Tony's got loads of food but he needs help picking it. And he will definitely want it to go to the right places. You could deliver some! But I guess your phone doesn't work so you can't call anyone to help?'

We wave Terry off after about half an hour.

We'd all sat in the cabin of his truck as he put the word out. Terry still had CB radio. It's sort of the same as a really powerful walkie-talkie. Apparently, Dad had always wanted one as a kid. Terry already had it tuned into Channel 19, he said, so all he had to do was press a button and any other truckers listening could join the conversation. They were all saying things like '10-4, understood' and '10–22 Angry Woods Farm' and so on. Terry said that since the screens went down, lots of minicab drivers and farmers and people on Harley-Davidson motorbikes had also started to use Channel 19. He said he would try and get as many as possible to come along and help get food from Uncle Tony and then make sure it got where it needed to go.

So we stand there as Terry slowly reverses his massive lorry back down the road on his way to Angry Woods Farm, and we jump back in the car. None of us knows what time it is, but from my tummy I guess I'd say it feels about three o'clock.

Wait. Maybe ten past.

I now realize just how scratched, dented and dirty our car really is. And, while Mum did a good job with the wheel, it's still bumping around and rattling. We're all thinking about what Terry said about food.

'Do you think it'll work?' says Mum, finding an ancient

CRACKER-
PIRANHAS
↓

pack of Ritz crackers in the glove compartment and throwing it towards me and Teddy. We rip it open and start devouring them like cracker-piranhas. Dad sighs and shrugs his shoulders.

'I mean, it's a long shot,' he says. 'But better than doing nothing.'

I don't get why they think it's a long shot. We hatched a plan, we did the plan, now we will see the plan work. That's my take on it anyway. I'm the sort of person who thinks there's no point in having a plan if the plan doesn't work. That doesn't mean there won't be surprises. I mean, take this trip, for example. The plan was to drive to Grandma's. And yes, there have been surprises. For example, Dad still smells and this morning he was chased by a pig. But we are still doing the plan. We are still on our way. We are still *doing something.*

'Shall I put some music on again?' asks Mum, and we all shout, 'Yeah!' as Dad turns left on to a bigger road. He's guessing now because we had to give Uncle Tony's map to Terry so he could find his way there.

The sky suddenly seems wider and full of clouds and it's like we're properly on our way to Grandma's at long last.

And we all loudly sing along to George Ezra and let the wind whip through the windows.

And we pass big fields.

And we wave at cows.

And we sing loudly.

There's something about the hum of the road and the smell of the grass that seems to make us all feel much lighter somehow.

And then suddenly Dad says, 'I don't believe it!' and turns the radio off.

He pulls quickly into a lay-by at the side of the road and we all get out of the car.

'Look,' says Mum. 'Stella, *look*!'

There are trucks coming this way. Lots of trucks. And minicabs. And people on motorbikes and in Land Rovers with little trailers rattling behind them. We know instinctively: this is because of us. Mum grabs my hand and squeezes it. They must be on their way to Angry Woods Farm to collect the food and take it to people who need it!

They whiz past and Dad can't help himself. He puts his arm in the air and pretends to be pulling an airhorn – like a big kid! – and then the trucks all start honking as they pass!

The people on bikes wave and Teddy is laughing hard now, so hard, and it makes us all so happy. Dad can't stop doing it.

Hoooonk!

Hooooooonk!

Dad can't stop smiling and shaking his head. He's sitting back in his seat; that's also what I notice. Yesterday morning, when we started out, it was like he couldn't get close enough to the steering wheel. I didn't realize his shoulders could go as low as they are now.

Mum has her window right down and is stretching her arm out to enjoy the sun.

Teddy is holding my hand and smiling. He loved all the trucks. He kept calling them 'Stella's Trucks'. He has been beaming at me like I am an absolute god, and it makes me laugh.

Mum looks at Dad and says, 'How long until we're there, do you think?'

'Well, we're behind by a long way,' he says. 'But I think if we just keep going at this sort of speed we'll be there tonight.'

Mum does half a smile. Do you know the type I mean? It sort of says, 'That's good news' but at the same time it doesn't.

I noticed one last night too when we did the fire. When we were out of the house. On the open road. Under the stars. Free. It's like the smile of someone who's happy, but maybe knows it won't last.

Some way up ahead, there is someone walking down the side of the road. He or she is wearing a red rain jacket even though it's not raining, and they're carrying a sign. When they hear us, they turn round and hold it up.

We have to get much closer before I can read it, but it says *GOING THAT WAY!*

I think it means they're going the same way we're going.

'No,' says Dad before Mum can say anything. 'We're not picking up a hitchhiker.'

But now we can see it's a kindly and very old lady with a cloud of white hair. She's wearing shorts and hiking boots and carrying a stick and she looks lost out here.

'But if we're going the same way . . .' says Mum.

'Nope!' says Dad, and we cruise past the lady.

'Dad!' I say. 'We all have to help each other! She might be on her way to see someone, just like we are! And she's like a million years old!'

'We can't,' says Dad. 'We've been held up enough already. Look, it's time to just get there now.'

'But, Dad!' I say because I really feel strongly about this. 'What about all the people who've helped us?'

'Eh?'

'What about the lady in the library with the books? Or the guy who pulled us out of the mud? What about Uncle Tony letting us stay over in his caravan and giving us petrol? What about Terry the Trucker man? Did the people on motorbikes and in minicabs teach us *nothing*? We are *all in this together,* Dad!'

Dad shuts his eyes for a split second.

Then he hits the brakes and we squeal to a halt dramatically.

I turn and wave at the lady, who waves her stick back.

Turns out I made a mistake because this is one really annoying hitchhiker.

CHAPTER NINE

'NO, that's not how you get there. You MISSED the turning, which I was VERY clear about,' yells Ellie, sitting right between me and Teddy and really squeezing us against the windows. 'Also, what on earth has happened to your car and WHAT is that smell?'

'That's Daddy,' says Teddy, and Dad blushes.

'Well, shall I turn round?' says Dad, in his best, most patient voice. 'Or is there another way to get there, Ellie? Only we've been driving quite a long time and

I'm a bit worried because we don't have a huge amount of petrol.'

We've been going AGES.

'That's not my fault,' says Ellie, sharply. 'This is *your* car. *You* missed the turning.'

I think Ellie thinks we must be some kind of taxi company or something. She has that loud confidence that I've noticed very posh people have where they think everyone must work for them in some capacity.

Ellie instructed us to take her to her house, which is apparently called Blackberry Manor and appears to be deep in some woods. She told us that she'd been given a lift into town, but had been late by 'just a few hours' for the taxi that was supposed to take her back. So he'd left. The way she told the story was like it was the taxi driver who'd behaved badly.

'Can't you go a little faster?' she says to Dad. 'You drive like an old lady.'

Dad accelerates by maybe two miles per hour just to shut her up.

'I miss driving,' she says. 'Haven't driven in years. Eyesight's gone to pot. Rotten luck! Can't see the road. Used to love it!'

That's sad, I think. That's why it's lucky we could help her.

'You know all this civil unrest is *mild rude word!* exciting,' she says, nudging me hard.

I can't believe she said that. This car does not usually

have rude words in it. Not unless Mum is driving.

'People fighting all over the place,' she says. 'I heard on the news that one man got a broken nose because he wanted the last packet of Coco Pops. Riots left, right and centre. Bank robberies. Petrol-station hold-ups. Anywhere there's cash.'

'What's a hold-up?' says Teddy.

'Nothing!' says Mum, clearly not wanting to worry him, but I'm pretty keen to know more.

'Yes, the country's on its knees,' says Ellie. 'Whole world is. And all because people can't watch Netflix or play Candy Crushers or whatever it's called.'

'Well, it's a little more complicated than that, Ellie,' says Mum. 'And maybe this is a conversation for another time . . .'

I don't know if anything Ellie is saying is true, but it sounds true. Though I also know that sometimes, when people can't get information, they start to make up their own.

'Anyway,' says Mum. 'Surely we're nearly at your home?'

'I've no idea,' asks Ellie. 'All looks the same to me. And I can barely see a thing.'

Dad starts to grip the steering wheel hard again, and Mum strokes his arm to calm him down.

'Are you sure this is the right way?' says Ellie, squinting.

'No!' says Dad. 'I thought you knew!'

'Are you sure you're even a taxi driver?'

'No!' says Dad.

'Well, where are we?' says Ellie.

'I have NO IDEA!' says Dad.

'You'd think a taxi driver might have some idea,' says Ellie, looking at me as if I'm going to back her up. 'Ah, look, here we are. I got us here in the end.'

Up ahead, a big brown sign says

'I don't believe it,' says Dad, as Mum unpacks the car. 'We were on our way. We had just enough petrol. And now look!'

The car conked out the second we stopped outside the front door of Blackberry Manor. We were out of petrol, the exhaust pipe was smoking and we'd lost three of our hubcaps since yesterday morning. Dad was going to have a job explaining the state of the car to his work, said Mum. It looked so bad that Dad had to push it round the corner of the main house because Ellie said it looked untidy out front and would make local property prices plummet.

Blackberry Manor was enormous. It had a long gravel driveway like in *Downton Abbey* and lots of windows everywhere. The door was the width of two normal doors and Ellie said it even had a Great Hall. A thought suddenly struck me. This really reminded me of Grandma's house.

'Do you know a lady called Nanette Bobcroft?' I ask Ellie.

'Where does she live?' says Ellie.

'Rendlesham,' I say. 'In Suffolk.'

'Never heard of her. Why?'

'Oh, she's my grandma. We're on our way to see her,' I say. 'We were supposed to be there by now.'

Ellie makes a face like I've said something wrong.

'And then I got in the way, did I? Drove you off course?'

'No!' I say because that's not what I mean, but it's like I've insulted her.

'Can I see the Great Hall?' I ask, trying to change the subject.

Ellie says no. She says none of us can come in because we might accidentally let all the dogs out. The dogs are not to be disturbed. This makes me sad because there are dogs around and now all I really want is to see them but it sounds like I'm not going to be allowed.

I guess my face must show how disappointed I am because Ellie takes another look at me, at all of us, tired and dirty and hopeless, and she says look, we can stay in her field, if we really have to.

Dad's face falls, but it gives us somewhere to stop while we figure out what to do about the car, so he thanks her. And Ellie goes in, and Dad's like, 'Surely there's *one* spare bedroom in a place this big? Surely she could have let us have *that*?'

But then there's a whole load of barking from what sounds like about fifty dogs and Ellie is coming outside again, pushing the door shut behind her.

'Normally, we run a camping business at the back. What do they call it again? "Glamping."'

'Oh yes?' says Mum, perking up.

'And, what with no one being able to look at our website, we don't have any bookings and consequently no guests. So you'll have the run of the place. There are some fresh towels there, in case any of you would like a *wash*?'

She stares hard at Dad when she says that.

'I'll send some food over. Do sleep well.'

The campsite wasn't like any campsite I'd seen before.

First off, forget the fire we lit in that lay-by. Here there was a proper big firepit for us to sit round. We got straight to work lighting it, even though the sun hadn't quite set yet.

And there was a big field for me and Teddy to run around in, with hay bales to jump off and roll around on.

There were alpacas in the field next to it, and bags

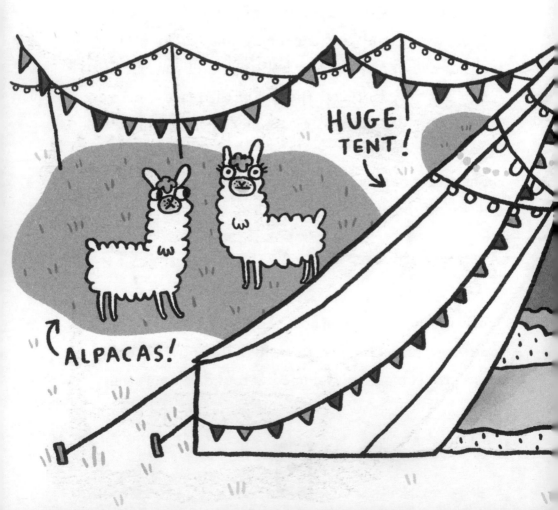

HUGE TENT!

ALPACAS!

of feed for us to give them.

And the tent was HUGE. It was covered in fairy lights and lanterns and the beds looked cosy, with thick duvets and the softest and fattest pillows possible.

Dad had looked gobsmacked when he saw that right

OUTDOOR BATHTUB!

outside the tent was a big outdoor bathtub. He threw his hands up to the clouds and yelled, 'Thank you!' and ran a giant bubble bath straight away, and afterwards he said he was the cleanest he'd felt in months!

Then a man had arrived on a golf cart, pulling a whole trolley of food from Ellie.

TRAILER OF FOOD

Ham, beef, chicken. Burgers for me and Teddy. Chocolate milkshakes and ice cream. Apart from some Ritz crackers, all I'd had was an egg at Uncle Tony's farm and I suddenly realized how hungry I was.

Everything was sort of . . . perfect.

'This was kind of the lady,' says Teddy.

'It's good to be kind,' I tell him, 'isn't it, Ted?'

And now we're sitting round the fire on this warm summer night and the stars are starting to poke through the sky. Teddy's in a fluffy white dressing gown, and it's just us – just the family, with the dry grass under our

feet – and I can't help but remind Dad of a few things.

'So, did you prefer getting sprayed by mud or being chased into a pond by a pig?'

Dad starts to laugh. A big surprising laugh. Like he'd been waiting to laugh about so many things for so long, but he'd had to get being annoyed out of the way first.

And we all laugh, until it slows and we sit in silence, watching the logs burn.

'Dad,' I say. 'Can I ask you something?'

'Anything, Stels,' says Dad.

'Did you fall out with Grandma the way Uncle Tony fell out with his sons?'

Mum raises her eyebrows, like she was not expecting that. But she doesn't deny it. She looks to Dad.

'I just mean because it seems like, even though you guys are busy with work and all that, and Grandma lives so far away, I just mean maybe it's weird we never, ever go there? And, like, it takes something mad like this screens thing to make you actually put us in a car and drive us there . . .'

Dad thinks for a bit and then nods.

And he says, 'I can barely even remember what it was about.'

I woke up the next morning when the cockerels started crowing.

Believe me, I know I made that sound  properly magical because who doesn't want to be woken up by a massive shouting bird, right? But have you ever heard one of them up close? One second everything is beautiful and peaceful and sleepy and the next it's like nature's held an airhorn up to your ear.

But the sun . . . the sun was magical. It streamed into the tent. We'd left it open in the night.

It must have rained while we were asleep too because I

could smell that amazing smell. You know the one? The one that just smells of earth and the ground and the water feeding the grass. The one that smells of the planet.

There were other smells too. Bacon was sizzling on a pan by the firepit. And there was the smell of aftershave or something drifting **BACON SANDWICH mmm** through the tent. Dad had got up early to have a shave with all the free toiletries.

I know she'd been a bit annoying at first, but finding Ellie was like striking gold. It gave us that one night we needed.

Teddy knew it too. I felt sorry for him. His routine was all out of whack. But a burger and a long sleep had been good for him.

'What time are we leaving, Dad?' I ask, as he hands out the bacon sandwiches.

'Whatever time you want,' he says. 'Because I don't know what time is or what time even means any more.

Everything is meaningless and yet meaningful. And those are my thoughts on this beautiful but weird morning.'

Dad doesn't usually have a second coffee and now I see why. But I know what he means. Everything felt so urgent at first. So confusing. Since we got to Ellie's, it's sort of felt like a Sunday.

'Do I have time to play with Teddy?' I ask.

I knew Ellie was watching us from the window as we ran around. She had a stern face and crossed arms, so I was worried she didn't want us running about the place, but she didn't stop us, so we just kept going.

It's when we're exploring the blackberry patches that she turns up right behind us, surrounded by eight dogs. Big ones. Tiny ones. Woofing and yapping.

I start petting them all straight away. I can't stop smiling. Which one would I choose, if one day I'm actually allowed one? A tiny dog leaps up at Teddy and licks him and Teddy screams with delight.

I think Ellie is pretending that she has work to do because she's carrying a pitchfork. I think she brought all her dogs out because she knew we'd like them. I think she just wants to talk.

'So where are you from?' she says, not quite looking at us.

'Mousehole,' I say. 'It's in Cornwall. Down by the sea.'

'I know Mousehole,' she says. 'Sacked by the Spaniards in 1595! Whole village burned down apart from one house!'

'It's still there,' I tell her.

'We always overcome!' says Ellie, looking into the distance. 'So, you will see your grandmother today. That's nice for you.'

'Do you have grandchildren?' I say.

'Yes, two,' she says. 'But they're in Australia.'

'What about your husband?' I say, and I immediately regret it.

Ellie says she had one a very, very long time ago, but that he had died. They had flown all over the world together. He used to be a pilot. He even flew Spitfires. Immediately, Teddy's fascinated because he knows all about Spitfires. Ellie says her husband had been one of the youngest ever pilots and had flown in the Second World War when he was just eighteen and he lived to be eighty-eight, so that taught Hitler a lesson, eh?

Ellie's face completely changes when she talks about him. She looks us in the eye the whole time. It's like we're just normal friends.

And then Dad gets here.

'Morning, Ellie. I was just wondering about petrol . . .'

'Do I look like someone who would have petrol?' she snaps. 'Gin, yes. Sherry, certainly. Champagne, at a push. But petrol?'

'Well . . . do you have the number for that taxi

company?' says Dad.

'No taxi company in their right mind is going to drive you to Rendlesham,' she says, like that is the craziest idea ever. 'It's at least two hours away.'

Dad sighs. The car is broken. We have no petrol. We can't get a taxi. We're stuck.

And then Ellie looks at Dad. Freshly cleaned but broken. Freshly shaved but helpless.

And she says, 'Why don't you just borrow my car?'

And Dad goes, 'But you said you haven't driven in years?'

And Ellie goes, 'I said I hadn't *driven*, not that I didn't keep my car. Of course I kept my car!'

And Dad goes, 'But why did you keep it?'

And Ellie says, 'Because, darling, you don't just get rid of a Rolls-Royce!'

This was the fanciest, sleekest, shiniest, most ridiculous and most *purple* car in the world.

It was so wide in the back you could slide around every time you turned a corner. I felt like we were all supposed to be wearing suits and caps or something. I felt like Meghan Markle or someone who'd won a competition on the radio.

This was the car that Ellie and her husband had driven, visiting their friends all over the country together. It obviously meant the world to her. Each week a member of her staff kept it 'polished and ticking over'. I couldn't believe she was lending it to us.

'Yes, well, needs must,' Ellie says, preparing to wave us off. 'Better that your grandmother isn't alone. Just make sure you return it!'

'Thank you for letting us stay,' I say, and she leans over to ruffle my hair. I don't know why grown-ups do that, but I guess you have to let them.

RUFFLING

And then Teddy does the most brilliant thing.

He reaches into his pocket and pulls out a present for Ellie.

'What's this?' she says, taking it.

And she's still staring at it as we drive away, polishing it on her cuff and holding this Royal Air Force badge close, and smiling. 'Just like you would do, Stella,' says Teddy, beaming at me.

And I squeeze his hand and tell him how proud I am to be his big sister.

POLISHING

CHAPTER TEN

'Wooooooooooo!' yells Mum from the front seat. 'Okay, let me drive now.'

'Absolutely not,' laughs Dad. 'If this car gets so much as a scratch, we'll have to sell our house to pay for it.'

'Come on!' says Mum. 'We'll get there so much faster with me behind the wheel!'

Dad laughs again. For a second I wonder what life was like for Mum and Dad when me and Teddy weren't here.

Were they always making jokes and messing about?

'Dad, what did you play as a kid?' I ask.

'What do you mean, Stels?' he says.

'Did you play Ding Dong Ditch?' I ask, thinking of Uncle Tony.

'No,' he says. 'Because I was not born in 1903. No, we played . . . Street Fighter 2. And Sonic the Hedgehog.'

'Sounds like you were on your screens a bit too much,' I say. 'Doesn't sound healthy.'

'We played football too. And sure, I guess we must have played Ding Dong Ditch.'

'Ding Dong Ditch?' says Mum. 'That's where you knock on people's doors and run off before they answer them? We used to call that Knock Down Ginger. That's naughty! I can't imagine you doing that!'

'Well, I did actually,' says Dad. 'And it was fun. I know it's naughty, but gosh, the adrenaline! Am I right, Stels?'

He looks at me in the rear-view mirror.

'Stella?'

I shrug at him.

'Wait – you've never played Ding Dong Ditch?'

Dad has found a small street in a little village just off the main road.

I look over the field next to it and I can see the rise of the motorway. It's completely empty. If we got on that road for just a few miles, we'd be able to cut out so much of the journey. A quick left after that and we'd be heading straight for Grandma's house. But I guess rules are rules.

We are crouching behind the Rolls-Royce as Dad gives us his team talk.

'Okay,' he says. 'So again, what we're about to do is naughty. But every kid needs to do it at least once in their life and I'm sad to say we have been failing you as parents if we have deprived you of this experience.'

'Things get busy,' I say, very understandingly.

'Well, we're not busy now,' says Dad. 'We're going to do one each. I'll take house number one. Stella, you take house number three. Mum and Teddy, you go for house number five.'

'And what do we do?' I ask because I like to get a real sense of the rules before I play a game. I read the rules of Scrabble five times before I committed to my first go.

'We walk up, we knock on the door – and then we run off!'

I can't believe Dad is about to do this. And, what's more, I can't believe he's about to do this with me. He'd never have done something like this in Mousehole.

'So, are we ready?'

We nod, and Mum has to put her hand over her mouth

to stop laughing, and we each walk up the path of a different house.

Dad looks serious, and cracks his knuckles and wiggles his fingers, like this requires real skill and aptitude (word of the month in May).

CRACK

I have started to tremble because this is not like me at all.

tee hee

This is the opposite of being a responsible member of society. I can't seem to walk normally. My back is all stiff and I can't remember how to bend my knees. But I am so excited.

Mum can't stop giggling.

We each reach a separate door and raise the doorknockers before looking at each other, ready to slam them down and run.

But then a middle-aged man in a cardigan opens the

door of the house Mum's at.

'Oh, HELLO!' yells Mum, surprised, which makes the man jump, and then she bursts out laughing in shock.

'*Now*, Stella!' yells Dad and he *KNOCK-KNOCK-KNOCKS* his door, so I do the same.

BANG BANG BANG!

'Aaaargh!' screams Mum, still laughing. 'Bye!'

Now we're all running for the car, and I'm starting to laugh with relief, but Dad trips over and goes head first into a bush because that just seems to be his life now.

As he gets up, the door of his house opens and he

stands up and waves at them.

'I'm just looking at this lovely bush!' he shouts, dusting mud off his shoulders.

'Ruuun!' yells Mum, and Dad laughs as he runs, and he shouts, 'Start the car!'

Dad's letting Mum drive?!

She leaps into the driver's seat and starts trying to crank the weird old gearstick thing, as I do Teddy's seatbelt. Dad dives in through the window.

The tyres spin as Mum hits the gas and we all laugh as the people outside their houses scratch their heads and wonder

who on earth this weird family is, and before we know it Dad is shouting, 'No!' as Mum makes a sharp turn and we bounce up on to the motorway that no one's allowed to use.

Mum cranks up the music on the radio and we zoom down the middle lane of the empty motorway in a purple Rolls-Royce which has old-fashioned dials and no screens so I can see clear as day that we're going *a hundred miles an hour* and now all you can hear is us cheering.

'Well, here we are then,' says Mum, who seems to have got quite good at driving a posh car like this. 'Rendlesham. I bet everyone is ready to stretch their legs, eh?'

I don't know why, but I feel nervous. Well, I do know why. I want this to go well for Dad. And so does Mum because she's holding his hand. I am sure things become very complicated when you're a grown-up, especially when you can't just use an emoji to explain how you feel.

After I've said hello to Grandma and had a Nesquik or something, I'll take Teddy out into the maze. Or into the orchard, where we can find the Story Tree and the fairy glade. Maybe I'll dress him up in a suit of armour or something.

Mum puts the indicator on – it's so loud! – and we turn into a short road that leads into the forest. At the end is a small cottage. It's got a little wooden bench outside and two square windows. What is this place?

'What are we doing here?' I ask.

'This is Grandma's house,' says Dad, like I'm being silly. 'You probably don't recognize it without the Skype ring noise.'

I look at it again. What does he mean? I don't recognize it at all.

Where are the turrets? Where's the pond?

We get out and Mum says she hopes Grandma is in because this would have been 'a hell of a journey otherwise' ('scuse her language). Dad peers through the window and he spots something.

'The teapot,' he says. 'It's steaming. She's in.'

So he takes a deep breath and knocks on the door.

Wait.

We all look at each other.

We smile.

Should we?

'Blinkin' kids!' yells Grandma at the top of her lungs when she opens the door and there's no one to be seen. 'That's the third time this week!'

'Surprise!' we all yell, jumping out from behind the tree.

HIDING BEHIND THE TREE

'Oh my days!' shouts Grandma, and now she's laughing and a bit shaky, and me and Teddy hug her hard.

'We were worried about you!' I say. 'And we couldn't remember your phone number and we didn't have it written down and we couldn't email you or text you or call you on Skype and we wanted to make sure you were okay and Dad committed a crime and fell in a pond and smelled really bad for a really long time and we lit a fire in a field!'

There was a lot I wanted to say, okay?

'Oh, *welcome*!' she says, and then she looks up at Mum and Dad.

And there's a moment where her and Dad just look at each other. Then she stretches her arms out wide and Dad falls into them and he almost completely swallows her in a giant hug and I think that everything *they* wanted to say was said in that hug and never needed to be said again.

'You came to rescue me!' says Grandma as she brings out my Nesquik to the back garden.

'We were worried about you,' I say. 'In case you needed help.'

'Oh, I've got my vegetable patches,' she says. 'I've got my tins.'

Grandma's added whipped cream and about four million marshmallows to my mug. She says she always made sure she had enough in her cupboard just in case I ever made it round.

'People my age know how to be ready for anything!' she says.

Her back garden is quite tiny. I remember it being the size of a football pitch.

'Do you remember the maze?' she says, and of course I do! But where is it? 'We used to put out cardboard boxes everywhere and build them together for hours. Wearing our tinfoil suits of armour.'

Cardboard boxes? Tinfoil?

'And the Story Tree?' Grandma says. 'Do you remember the Story Tree?'

I do, but I can't see it . . .

She points at the big green garden umbrella in the corner.

'We used to sit under that and make up our own stories, before we got the paddling pool out and then jumped in the—'

'The pond!' I say, remembering.

All these memories I have – of being little and stomping through big marshes and hiding in forests and building dens and finding fairy houses – Grandma gave them all to me and made them real.

'There's nothing like playing,' she says. 'You can do

anything and be anyone. You can make the world your own!'

It's nice to have some memories that could never, ever have actually happened the way I thought. Something unrecorded. It's like magic. It's like a present.

'Did Dad use to play like that?' I ask her.

'Oh my, oh yes,' says Grandma. 'We used to put cereal boxes on our backs and pretend to be divers or astronauts. Oh, it was such fun. Can you imagine? Your dad could play for hours. He would just laugh and laugh and create incredible worlds!'

Hang on.

'What – *my* dad?'

'Yes,' says Grandma. 'Wait. I can *show* you!'

We have had to wait until the sky got a little bit darker and

Grandma could find all the things she needed from the attic.

I still didn't see how she could show us Dad as a kid. I still didn't really believe Dad ever was a kid. Though I suppose seeing him and Mum singing and acting like they were young and then even playing Ding Dong Ditch is a clue that he must have been young at some stage.

Mum and Dad have been giggling in the kitchen, I think because they'd opened some wine (uh-oh) while they chopped some of Uncle Tony's vegetables for a sauce, and now we have a big steaming bowl of pasta for us all to eat in the garden. We're sat under the Story Tree, lit by yellow light bulbs, and I take two big bits of garlic bread. One for me and one for Teddy.

THE STORY TREE

PASTA

GARLIC BREAD ♡

Then Grandma brings all these weird bits of equipment out.

'I found the old films!' she says.

'Oh no,' says Dad.

'We can't watch films, Grandma,' I say. 'The screens are all gone, remember?'

She laughs.

'We haven't always needed screens,' she says. 'Not electronic ones anyway!'

And she unfolds this big white sheet on a tripod and it's like a sort of cinema screen. Then she puts together an old 'projector' that looks like something from before time began, but which Grandma says is actually from 1981, which I have to say sounds like a made-up year.

'What's that?' I say, pointing to a square orange box in her hand. She doesn't answer, but opens it up and I can see a roll of plastic inside, which she threads into the projector.

And then . . .

Up on the screen, in very tiny shorts – there's a little boy

Grandma claims is Dad!

'Awwwww!' says Mum, and she ruffles the real-life Dad's hair and cuddles into him.

The colours are all a bit weird and there's no sound apart from the whirr of the projector but, yeah, I think that's my dad!

'That's Daddy!' I tell Teddy. 'In the very tight Superman T-shirt!'

And then there's Grandma, with red hair, and she's wearing cardboard boxes on her back and pretending to

be an evil robot! And they're laughing and playing and I don't even need to hear what they're saying because I'm just blown away by all the . . .

The what?

The love.

Next to me, Dad puts his arm round Grandma and kisses her on the head.

And he cuddles her a little more when the camera turns round and there's Grandad.

TO END WITH

The screens still haven't come back, of course. But you know that.

Mum says everyone needs to learn how to live in a different world, and Grandma says she's right because things always change.

But it's a world I'm cool with.

We're going to stay with Grandma the whole of the summer.

She says every day is going to be a play day. Of course at first this panics me because as you know I do enjoy a rigorously structured timetable. But she says by playing, we'll learn. She's going to teach us everything she knows. Things we wouldn't learn if the screens came back, or from an online lesson, or from what she calls the Google Machines.

We're going to get dirty every day, and we're going to get out of breath, and we're going to grow flowers and bake bread and invent stories and we're going to talk.

And every week we're going to do something special for someone we don't really know at all. The way Uncle Tony and Ellie and the people we met did something for us.

And we're going to make sure we remember to pay for those fish and chips from that rude woman at that pub.

Most importantly, every Sunday will still be Bobcroft
Family Film Night. But now the films will be ones we
make ourselves, ones we watch while eating great big
bowls of pasta around a table in the garden together.

We can't take pictures on our phones any more. But
I blink, hard, whenever I find a moment to remember.
There are so many.

And just before I go, because I think I've given you

the whole story now, Dad said that he thinks that in the past week we've made more memories together than we ever did before. So he said that he and Mum had been talking, and it was time to make some more. And that if I promised that I would be responsible for the walks, and for the feeding, and the care, we could do it this week.

So we're going to go to the rescue centre, and we're actually going to get a puppy.

I'm going to call her Grandma.

Acknowledgements

Huge thanks to Jane Griffiths, Ali Dougal, Sam Swinnerton, Jesse Green, Rachel Denwood, Laura Hough, Eve Wersocki Morris and all the greats at Simon & Schuster – as a reward, you all get an extra hour of screen time this weekend!

Robert Kirby, I'm taking your phone away, I'm afraid.

All Hail Gemma Correll!

And big thanks to my three inspirations: Elliot, Clover and Kit. Let's do a road trip!